T

When the CHIEF fell in LOVE

Kashmiriyat... Jamhooriyat... Insaniyat...

HINDUSTANIYAT

Published by
Fi NGERPRINT!
An imprint of Prakash Books India Pvt. Ltd.

113/A, Darya Ganj, New Delhi-110 002,
Tel: (011) 2324 7062 – 65, Fax: (011) 2324 6975
Email: info@prakashbooks.com/sales@prakashbooks.com

facebook www.facebook.com/fingerprintpublishing
twitter www.twitter.com/FingerprintP
www.fingerprintpublishing.com

Copyright © 2018 Prakash Books India Pvt. Ltd.
Copyright Text © Tuhin A Sinha

This is a work of fiction. Names, characters, places and incidents are either product of the author's imagination or are used fictitiously, and any resemblance to any actual person, living or dead, events or locales is purely coincidental.

All rights reserved. No part of this publication may be reproduced, stored in a retrieval system or transmitted in any form or by any means, electronic, mechanical, photocopying, recording or otherwise (except for mentions in reviews or edited excerpts in the media) without the written permission of the publisher.

ISBN: 978 93 8653 897 0

Processed & printed in India by HT Media Ltd, Noida

For Mumma,
Life can never be the same without you,
Your presence, though, feels stronger with every passing day.

CONTENTS

Prologue
7

PART ONE:
Vihaan: Interrupted Love
13

PART TWO:
Zaira: A Chequered Life
67

PART THREE:
Vihaan: Past Imperfect Future Tense
133

PART FOUR:
Vihaan: Kashmiriyat, Jamhooriyat,
Insaniyat . . . Hindustaniyat!
163

Epilogue
222

An excerpt from *Resurgent Paradise*
229

Acknowledgement
245

PROLOGUE
New Delhi, September 2016

It was an unusual day where the sun and the clouds seemed to engage in an unexpected one-upmanship battle over supremacy and the valley looked both sunny and cloudy intermittently. In an eerie sort of a way, the fickle weather was symbolic of the uncertainty that seemed to have become a part of Kashmir's existence.

Ripping this uncertainty aside, the cavalcade of Vihaan Shastri, India's youngest defence minister ever, sped through the highway towards the army camp in Gurez, hardly a kilometre away from the Line of Control. Barely twelve hours ago, Gurez had been just another quaint little border town in Kashmir. Located high up in the Himalayas, about 123 kilometres from Srinagar, it had no idea that it would suddenly invoke patriotic fervour in millions of people across the country.

The previous night, four militants, heavily armed with AK-47 rifles had stormed into the administrative building and the store complex of the Twelfth Infantry Brigade, killing eighteen soldiers and injuring as many before being gunned down. Vihaan had been hurriedly flown into Srinagar in a special Indian Air Force aircraft, along with the national security advisor. They met the injured soldiers at the Army Base Hospital in Srinagar before heading off to the army camp in Gurez by road to take stock of the situation.

Vihaan looked outside the window of his speeding car. He was so stressed that the beautiful scenery hardly registered upon him. With prime-time television anchors demanding retaliation, Gurez remained on tenterhooks even as the Kishanganga river flowed by serenely, perhaps wondering about the shape and the consequences of a befitting revenge.

"Has any terror outfit claimed responsibility yet?" Vihaan turned to Mahesh Rana, his personal secretary, seated next to him.

"Not yet. Initial intelligence reports suggest the involvement of Jaish-e-Muhammad and Hizbul Mujahideen. A section of the Hurriyat may have been privy to the strike. The ammunition recovered from the slain terrorists had Pakistani military markings," Rana replied with his trademark calm demeanour.

Vihaan mulled over the possibilities that could play out over the next forty-eight hours. "Has our Director General of Military Operations (DGMO) conveyed our concerns to his Pakistani counterpart?" he asked.

"Yes, he did. But you know what their template response has always been, that India's claims are unfounded and premature, and they asked for actionable intelligence. The DGMO will brief you in detail at the camp."

Vihaan looked out of the window again as his cavalcade sped past small garrisons to enter Gurez. Bricks and barracks blended with ease in this nondescript border town. Why has Kashmir remained a festering wound that refuses to heal for the past seven decades? Vihaan began to wonder. Who is to be blamed? Jawaharlal Nehru? The Abdullahs? Maharaja Hari Singh? Was the Indian leadership even capable of resolving the issue?

At this point, Vihaan's phone rang again. It was his sixteen-year-old daughter, Tia, who studied at the Welhams' Girls School in Dehradun. She had already called him twice before, but he had been unable to pick up.

"Hi Tia," Vihaan answered the call quickly, aware that he would be reaching the army camp any moment now.

"Dad! I've been following the news channels. Where are you? Are you okay?"

"Yes *beta*. I am in Gurez. I'm fine. I'll call you in the evening."

"Dad, did you have your meal?"

Every time Tia propped up this innocent query, it would make Vihaan go weak. He missed her so much.

"I did, *beta*. I'll call you later. You take care."

When the cavalcade entered the army base camp moments later, the army personnel were lined up on both sides of the entrance to welcome Vihaan, the man at the helm of their affairs. This was the first time a defence minister had ever visited this border town. The army chief, already in Gurez, recieved Vihaan. After a quick formal greeting, the briefing started. Vihaan, however, remained preoccupied, seething with indignation. He mulled over possible revenge options. This time, he wanted India to retaliate in a way she had never done before. The PM had already tweeted that India wouldn't take this misadventure lying low and would reply in a language that the enemy understood.

"I share your anguish," Vihaan addressed the army personnel as the briefing ended, "but you have to give me the best retaliation options. We need more than the preliminary details. We need a solid plan. Until then, take care."

"Sir, it's time to take you to the Srinagar airport," Mahesh whispered. Vihaan nodded at the men assembled in the briefing room before following the army chief out towards his waiting car.

***

After landing at the Delhi airport, Vihaan drove straight to 7, Lok Jan Kalyan Marg, to brief the prime minister, Vaibhav Patel, about his Gurez visit.

"This time, we will give it back to Pakistan. Let's meet again the day after, once the army chief gives us his recommended options," Patel noted, grim and stern-faced. Patel, though just two years into office, was already being viewed as India's most decisive and far-sighted leaders. The home minister, Siddharth Gupta, with whom Vihaan did not enjoy the best of equations, was also present in this meeting.

By the time Vihaan returned home, it was almost midnight. He wondered if he should call Tia but decided against it; she must have slept off. Vihaan took a quick shower. Then, as he sat over a bowl of mushroom soup, his usual meal every time he had dinner this late, he flippantly gazed through social media to gauge people's reactions. The outrage was collective and unanimous.

Stressed and hyper, Vihaan tried to switch off by listening to some classical music. Meanwhile his cook, Raghu, brought out a few documents and put them on the table in front of him.

"Madhab Sir had asked me to show these to you."

They were the usual letters and official papers which Madhab, his assistant personal secretary, would leave for his attention.

"I'll see them tomorrow," he said.

No sooner had he said this than a card caught Vihaan's attention. He picked it up for a closer look, even as a confused frown dotted his visage.

It was an invitation card, sent by a publisher for the release of the best-selling author Zaira Bhat's new book, *A Chequered Life* . . .

Vihaan read the invitation again, and again, a gamut of conflicting emotions covering his face.

PART ONE

VIHAAN: INTERRUPTED LOVE

CHAPTER ONE
Delhi, December 1990

There is something mystical about Delhi Decembers, especially if you are in North Campus. The place suddenly becomes intensely vibrant, what with students soaking in the winter sun and chirping all around. The eclectic colours of their winter wear adds to the natural spirit of bonhomie as well.

This was my third year in Delhi and I lived in the hostel of one of Delhi University's top colleges—the Hindu College. It was that time of the year when everyone was in a tizzy over the annual college festival, Mecca, a three-day event that would draw in heaps of students from all over Delhi to participate in multiple contests and activities. In fact, for a Hinduite, and more so for a hosteller, these three days were marked on the calendar right at the start of the academic year. And in the weeks and days immediately preceding the event, the excitement would spiral exponentially. For many of the Hindu hostellers who spent most of the year lurking around outside girls' colleges, this festival provided the hope of bumping into pretty girls on home turf.

For me, the excitement that year was offset by a tinge of melancholy which I could attribute to two distinct causes. The first was the overall communal disturbance in the country. In fact, 1990 will probably be remembered as the most politically turbulent year in independent India. Right from the mass exodus of Hindus from the Kashmir valley at the start of the year, to the anti-reservation stir which led to many students immolating themselves, and finally, the Ram Janmabhoomi movement, the year was marked with political disturbances and violence.

The second cause was more personal. Two and half years ago, when I had set out for Delhi from the small town of Benaras, I had expected more from the city. While Benaras did have a top-class university in Banaras Hindu University (BHU), which my father would have preferred for me to go to, I found Delhi ambition-igniting. I guess there was something aspirational about being around the structures of power which mattered to the country. In fact, once in a while, I actually enjoyed going to the Rashtrapati Bhawan and the Parliament House to just take a closer look at these iconic structures. I found it difficult to decipher this craving in those days, but as a student of History Honours, I was perhaps distinctly curious about the history of places and structures, and more so about the creators of these historical structures.

However, coming back to the second reason for my being melancholic that year, I had been fairly certain when I first landed in Delhi that this city would give me my first steady girlfriend. But, until now, I had had no luck on this score! And it had begun to quietly frustrate me.

***

Chapter One: Delhi, December 1990

It was afternoon. The college festival was well underway, but the crowd response this time was so low that I had walked out of the hall and was walking through the campus garden all alone. The weather was overcast, adding to the gloom. I felt unusually forlorn, like I have seldom felt in Delhi, almost wanting to board the first train home. Just then, I heard a voice shouting out for me from behind.

"Vihaan! Vihaan! I've been looking all over for you."

It was Suraj, my roommate. "What happened?" I asked, disenchanted.

"*Arre yaar*, you know the poetry competition is about to start in the main hall. I want you to be there."

Suraj was studying English Literature and had a penchant for poetry. In fact, he'd recite his creations to me every now and then. I found them good, but I wasn't sure if I was qualified enough to give him the right feedback. Nonetheless, sensing his nervousness about the contest, I knew I ought to be there for him.

As I walked inside the hall, I managed to find a seat in the fourth row and sat down. One after the other, the participants came on the stage and recited their poems. It all seemed somewhat boring as none of the poems had anything extraordinary to hold my attention. I was about to get up and leave when there was an announcement:

"And now, I request Zaira Bhat, our next speaker, to come on stage and recite her creation."

A slim girl with long auburn hair, turquoise eyes, sharp eyebrows and raised cheekbones, and with vulnerability written all over her countenance, appeared on stage. She was wearing an off-white salwar kameez with a maroon pashmina shawl draped across her shoulders. The image of her was simply so captivating that I just stared. And then, in a somewhat husky, accented voice, which may have been modulated to suit the mood of her poem, she recited words that created magic and left me mesmerised.

> *It has been a while*
> *since I've seen you smile.*
>
> *The sunrays from snow-clad mountains*
> *are looking for you.*
>
> *The majestic look of the Dal*
> *at twilight is losing it's hue*
>
> *I am lost in the woods,*
> *pine trees still whispering your name.*
>
> *I am searching for the missing pieces of my soul.*
> *But I am afraid they may have perished with you.*
>
> *It has been a while*
> *since I've seen you smile . . .*

I could sense the hurt in her words, which, combined with the innocence and the eloquence, seemed to draw me in effortlessly. I wanted to enter the world she was talking of—the land of snow-capped mountains and the frozen lake with the shikaras. I could feel an instant connection with her and I found it rather intriguing.

But I was not the only one bowled over by this young poetess' charm. In fact, as she walked down the stage, quite a few enthralled people surrounded her, causing quite a distraction in the hall. I too, wanted to meet her, but before I could reach her, she had become invisible. Perhaps she had left quickly in order to avoid being mobbed. I felt restless. I wanted to meet her. But I had no clue why or for what.

***

At around seven-thirty that evening, when I walked back into the hostel room, Suraj was understandably furious at me: I had abruptly left the hall in the afternoon after that girl's performance, not waiting for his turn. Besides, I had been incommunicado for the next four hours—well, in those days, there were no cell phones and being out of sight meant being out of contact.

"But where the hell were you?" Suraj literally roared at me.

I felt sheepish telling him what had happened. Besides, did I myself know what had really happened? All I knew was that I had behaved really strangely, like I had never behaved before.

"For God's sake will you tell me what you've been up to?" Suraj shouted again.

I recollected then, how, like a man in a daze, I had walked out of the hall and the college as I desperately tried locating Zaira Bhat. It had been my bad luck that the announcer hadn't mentioned the name of her college, like he had in the case of the other contestants. Therefore, assuming that she belonged to one of the two girls' colleges in North Campus—Daulat Ram and Miranda House—and that she was a hosteller, I even tried to find her outside these colleges, hanging out there with another friend of mine. When it didn't work, I made a few specific enquiries from the girls walking in and out of these colleges, about whether someone called Zaira Bhat lived in the hostel or not. But I found out nothing and only ended up spending a good four hours trying to catch another glimpse of Zaira.

"What's wrong with you?" Suraj demanded, looking baffled.

I shrugged. I didn't know what was wrong with me, but something was terribly amiss for sure.

"And what will you do if you meet her? Kidnap her?"

I didn't have an answer to that question. I couldn't sleep that night. Images of Zaira on stage, her eyes, her words, her expression—they were all so alluring. They almost seemed to invite me to unravel her, like there was a story in her, waiting to be told.

I must have managed to finally fall asleep around six-thirty in the morning, only to be woken up around eight by bright sunlight streaming in through the window. Suraj was already up and reading the newspaper.

"Riots have broken out in Mirzapur and a few other districts in Uttar Pradesh," he said, keeping himself immersed in the paper.

I remained lost and disinterested.

"The government has imposed Section 144 across Uttar Pradesh."

Silence.

"Indraprastha College," he muttered, still from behind the newspaper.

"Sorry?" I asked, confused.

"I am talking about Zaira Bhat. She is from IP College and she stays in the hostel."

"Whatttt?!!!!!" I jumped up, excited.

Suraj then informed me that he had found out about Zaira from the head of the Literary Society of our college as she had a detailed list of all the participants of the poetry competition.

Chapter One: Delhi, December 1990

I hugged Suraj hard, almost making him fall off the chair. I knew then that either by choice or compulsion, I would have Suraj support me in my quest to find Zaira. Not for nothing was he my best buddy!

***

I landed outside IP College that very evening at around six, Suraj by my side. IP College was a good half-hour away from North Campus by bus. Being winter, it was already dark by the time we got there. Standing too close to the college gate would have invited suspicion or censure, or possibly both. Hence, we stood about 50 metres away from the gate, in front of the few food stalls that were lined up there.

"Are you looking for someone?" one of the hawkers asked us, smiling indulgently.

We shook our heads.

"Don't worry. Most girls come out for a quick evening bite to one of these stalls," he reassured us, his smile intact.

We ordered a plate of *pani puri* to begin with, our eyes fixed on the college gate. Ten minutes later, with no sign of Zaira yet and with a couple of girls staring at us suspiciously, we were forced to order another plate of *pani puri*. Twenty minutes later, with even more girls watching us with suspicion, we ordered two cups of tea, followed by a few samosas to prolong our stay.

Half an hour later, there was still no trace of Zaira. Two of the girls who were standing nearby, walked up to us then.

"Are you looking for someone?" one of them asked.

We introduced ourselves, stressing on the name of our college. "We're looking for Zaira Bhat," I replied nervously.

The two girls looked at each other before one of them replied. "She doesn't come out after its dark."

"W-w-why?" I asked, curious.

"She normally goes out only when her father sends a car. Her family faces a security threat in Kashmir and they are over-cautious about her safety here."

I looked helplessly as the two girls walked away. I knew I wouldn't see Zaira, not that evening and not that easily, but at the same time, I felt more determined than before to enter her world. Never before had intrigue seemed so inviting to me.

That night, Suraj tried in vain to dissuade me from pursuing Zaira any further. It led to a huge argument between us, with him refusing to be a part of my efforts anymore, but I remained stubborn.

The next evening, I landed at IP College all alone, more determined than ever to find Zaira.

"I am Imran Khan, Zaira Bhat's school friend from Kashmir," I informed the security guard at the hostel gate, faking a confidence I didn't feel. Thankfully, one didn't have to furnish an Aadhar card for verification in those days.

As the guard informed the hostel warden over the intercom and I waited for a reaction, I bit my nails in sheer nervousness. Agreed, 'Imran Khan' was an extremely common name and there was a high likelihood of someone by that name being Zaira's friend, but what if there wasn't one? What would I do then? Was I prepared for the consequences?

"Zaira is not in the hostel," the guard said, forcing me to snap out of my nervous thoughts. "She has gone to her local guardian's place."

Chapter One: Delhi, December 1990

I breathed a sigh of relief. I didn't know why exactly I wanted to meet Zaira, but while not meeting her didn't seem like an option anymore, I hadn't really prepared for the moment when I would actually face her.

As I turned to leave, I bumped into Ruchi, a girl from my school in Benaras, who was two years my junior and who happened to stay in the IP College hostel now. One thing led to another and as we stood chatting outside the hostel gate, I ended up telling her how I had wanted to meet Zaira and discuss something.

"Well, Zaira can be unpredictable," Ruchi said. "She stays here for only half the days and keeps going away every now and then."

"Where?" I asked inquisitively.

Ruchi shook her head. Before leaving, I gave Ruchi my hostel phone number and requested her to call and let me know whenever Zaira was back in the hostel next.

For the next couple of days, I didn't make any effort whatsoever to either meet Zaira or find out more about her. I also did not get the call from Ruchi, which I had been expecting. And yet, thoughts of Zaira wouldn't leave me alone. Why was her family under a security threat? Why and where did she disappear every now and then?

"She seems to be like a sweet poison. Beware of her," Suraj cautioned me.

"Huh," I grunted.

"Why do you want to invite trouble in your life? She could be a ter—"

My annoyed expression prevented Suraj from completing the word.

***

Two weeks went by and the new year, 1991, set in. Of course I still thought about Zaira many times every day. Yet, I felt that I was somehow more realistic now. I had almost begun to believe that I would never meet her again. And then, I got an unexpected call from Ruchi on the hostel landline—Zaira was back in the college hostel.

That evening, I landed up outside Zaira's hostel as Imran Khan once again. This time, I had managed to drag Suraj with me.

"Are you crazy? What will you tell her when she comes and sees you are not Imran?" Suraj had been babbling nervously all the way.

I didn't say anything, but for some unknown reason, I was brimming with confidence.

Zaira arrived at the hostel gate a little later, looking ravishing, but also perplexed. A female hosteller friend was accompanying her.

"Imran? Do I know you?" she queried, looking at me curiously.

"Hi, I am Vihaan," I said, smiling.

"But I was told it's Imran . . ."

I explained then how I had taken a chance and used the alias as I hadn't been sure if she would have come to meet me otherwise.

Zaira looked annoyed. "But who are you? And what do you want from me?" she demanded.

"Well, I heard you recite your poem at Mecca . . . I-I, ahem, I couldn't figure out what was more mesmerising, your persona or your words," I said sheepishly. "I felt an unusual connection with you, with your words . . . I can't seem to explain it well, but something has made me reach out to you."

Chapter One: Delhi, December 1990

"Thank you for the appreciation," she said somewhat nonchalantly. By now, her annoyance seemed to be giving way to amusement.

"And by the way, this is my friend, Suraj." I turned to introduce Suraj, only to realise he had vanished, leaving me all alone.

Seeing my confusion, the girls burst out laughing.

"What is he really up to?" Zaira's friend mumbled to her.

"Umm... Zaira, can I talk to you alone, just for a moment?" I asked hesitatingly.

The girls exchanged a look before Zaira stepped aside, her friend still visible, just a few feet away from us.

"Well, what do you want from me?" Zaira asked me sternly.

"Well, to begin with, your company and friendship..." She looked bemused even as I continued. "I want to know more about you, about your world. I want to hear your voice more often. I want to be with you."

"And then?" she asked, her face virtually expressionless, giving me no hint whatsoever of what she was thinking.

"Well..." I hesitated, "I am a very simple guy. As we become friends and if all goes well, I might just want to spend my entire life with you."

She looked stunned when I said this. "Are you here to propose marriage?!" she asked incredulously.

"Ya... n-n-no..." I stuttered.

There was pin drop silence for a few moments. Zaira looked shocked and offended, leaving me jittery. Then she burst out laughing. Her friend walked up to us, seeing her laugh like that.

"You know what Renu? This guy wants to discuss a lifelong companionship plan with me! And to think of it, he doesn't know me at all!"

"I want to get to know you. How much time does it take anyway to know somebody?" I shot back, trying to sound confident.

Zaira's laughter ceased as she gave me a serious, punctuated look. "To know me, even a lifetime may fall short." And grabbing her friend's hand, she began to walk away.

As I saw her move away from me, I recited a few lines from the poem Zaira had recited at Mecca.

She stopped and turned around, giving me a surprised look before laughing dismissively and walking away.

At that moment, I told myself, "The tougher you make the pursuit, the more I feel destined to embark upon a journey to find you."

***

The rules of romantic engagement way back in the '80s and '90s, before the advent of social and electronic media, were radically different. They call it stalking now, but in those days, just following a girl you liked and making eye contact with her would signal a lot. It was a definite expression of interest in her, without being offensive in the least. And hence, I embarked upon a hot pursuit of Zaira, aiming for moments of 'eye contact'.

I would go and stand outside Zaira's hostel during visiting hours, hoping that I could catch a glimpse of her when she came out. After two failed attempts, I got lucky on the third day. Zaira came out with her friend, Renu. When she saw me, all I could manage was a hesitant smile before she glared at me and hurriedly walked away with Renu.

I continued parking myself outside Zaira's college for the

next two days, much to Suraj's chagrin—he had almost stopped talking to me by then. I too, had begun to lose hope; besides, this stupidity was taking away a lot of my study time.

On the second day, as I stood at the bus stop waiting to board a bus back to North Campus, I saw Renu get down from a bus which had stopped at the same bus stop. Call it divine intervention or pure luck, but as she alighted from the bus, for a moment she stood right in front of me. On both the occasions when I had seen Zaira outside her hostel, I had felt that Renu, for some reason, seemed to have a softer attitude towards me than her friend did. Perhaps she was used to seeing boys fall for Zaira all the time and she felt sorry for them. Whatever it was, as she turned to leave, on an impulse, I blurted out from behind, "I love your friend. I really love her . . . just let her know this. Please."

She turned around, looking surprised. "Don't waste your time on her," she said after a beat. "She is hard to love."

"All I want is a few meetings with Zaira," I said. "She will realise that I really love her . . ." I could see Renu was in two minds. "Please . . ."

"Tomorrow, 3 p.m., we're going out to watch a movie at Batra," she said, surprising me, before adding, "But you better behave yourself there or it might be the last chance you get."

I nodded, controlling my excitement.

Batra Cinema used to be a famous landmark and a popular hang-out spot for college kids in North Campus. Located in the heart of Dr. Mukherjee Nagar, a prime refugee settlement area, this place used to buzz with activity almost all day long. Evenings were livelier with multiple eateries fuelling the young crowd's taste buds.

I reached Batra Cinema the next afternoon at half past two sharp, dragging Suraj with me. The movie being screened was *Baaghi: A Rebel For Love*, starring Salman Khan and Nagma. Now the plan I had in mind was this: Suraj would get into the ticket counter queue immediately after Zaira and her friends. That was our best chance of getting seats right next to the girls.

When Zaira and her friends arrived, I moved a little distance away so they wouldn't see me. Suraj, meanwhile, went and stood right behind them in the ticket queue, and for a change I actually got lucky! We got seats right next to them.

Minutes before the movie was to start, Suraj and I walked into the hall and Zaira discovered, much to her shock, that the guy seated next to her was me!

"Youuu?!" she exclaimed.

"Yeah, why? I've got the ticket," I mumbled.

Before she could react further, the movie began. Zaira pretended to be absorbed by the movie completely, but I could sense her distraction.

It was an obsessive love story, much along the lines of how mine was seeming to shape up. Quite obviously, we didn't interact through the movie, but during the interval I offered to get the girls popcorn. Before Zaira could respond, Renu grabbed the offer.

"Oh yeah, that would be nice!"

Even as I got up to get the popcorn, I heard Zaira grumbling to Renu about how "these guys could land up right next to them!"

Post interval, Zaira seemed more accepting of my presence for some reason. As she nibbled on the popcorn and a romantic song played out on the screen, I grew a bit gutsy and whispered to her, "Can I ask you out on a date?"

Chapter One: Delhi, December 1990

My query was met with an angry stare and with Zaira and Renu exchanging their seats, making Renu sit next to me.

"I told you to behave yourself," Renu mumbled to me, apparently amused.

And so, the end result of this contrived movie date was nothing but a damp squib!

***

A week later, IP College had its annual festival. There was no way I was going to miss it, especially when I had learnt that a poetry contest was going to be one of the key events of the festival. In fact, the annual festival of girls' colleges was the only opportunity in the year when boys could enter these sacred grounds. All they needed to carry was their college identity cards!

So there I was, seated in the second row from the front, witnessing the poetry contest at the IP fest. I waited impatiently for almost half an hour for the announcement of that one name which could make my heart race. And when it was made, I could feel my adrenalin rush like never before.

When Zaira came on stage, gorgeous as always, attired this time in black, she once again recited a poem of love, longing, and loss, making me wonder if these were what defined her. Such was the conviction with which she recited the words that it made the entire audience go still. When the poem ended, it left everyone in the audience spellbound for a few seconds and there was pin drop silence in the hall, until someone somewhere started clapping and broke the spell.

I snapped out of Zaira's magic as she left the stage to the sound of thunderous applause. I rushed out to catch her before she left, but I couldn't see her anywhere. I tried locating her, and even Renu, in the campus for the next one hour, but I just couldn't find them. Once again Zaira had slipped right through my fingers.

That evening when I returned to my hostel, I felt frustrated. Why was I chasing something that seemed so determined to elude me? What kind of a mad infatuation was this? Was it some strange karmic connection that was holding me in its grip? Why was I allowing myself to be degraded thus? Where had my ego suddenly vanished? Was I really in love? Or was it just the challenge of the chase that had me behaving like a fool?

I lay awake that night, tossing and turning on the bed, anger seeping into me, torturing my mind with a hundred questions and doubts. As hours went by, it seemed to me that I was bracing up for some kind of an explosion, only I had no clue what it would be.

The whole of the next day passed in a literal daze. I found myself filled with a nervous energy that made it impossible for me to focus on anything, and come evening, I landed up once again outside Zaira's hostel during the visiting hours. I was brimming with a confidence, or rather an assertiveness that I found difficult to decipher. I wasn't my normal self and I wasn't exactly sure what I would do. But I knew that this time if I did see Zaira, I wouldn't let her just pass me by.

I don't know how much time elapsed before I saw Zaira step out with three other girls. But when I spotted her, I ran, rather charged towards her and stood in front of her. She and her friends were obviously taken aback by my behaviour. My sleep-starved eyes and the ferociously intense expression on my face must have made me look ominous. Before Zaira or her friends could really make out what I was up to, I went down on my knees and proposed to her, right then and there.

Chapter One: Delhi, December 1990

"Zaira, I love you from the bottom of my heart . . ."

They were all rightly stunned.

"I love everything about you . . . the way you look, the way you talk, walk, everything. You are every bit the girl I want to spend my life with . . ."

By now, Zaira's friends couldn't hold back their grins anymore. Zaira, though, looked flummoxed. People who were passing us by had all gathered around us to see the drama. My eyes, however, were focussed only on Zaira, my heartbeat thumping in anticipation of her reaction. And there it was!

"Will you just get up and get lost?!" she screamed at the top of her voice, jolting me completely. "What the hell are you up to? Do you know me at all? Do I know you? Why the hell have you been stalking me?!"

Zaira's shouting attracted more people and a bigger crowd converged there. They all looked at me aghast, as though I had tried to molest Zaira. The two security guards stationed at the hostel gate came running and were about to forcibly pull me away when I shot back with surprising ferocity.

"Ms. Zaira Bhat, it is okay to spurn my love. But you know what, you don't deserve to be loved. You don't have the basic sensitivity to handle a situation like this. I'm sorry I thought you were more mature than this. But now I know your poems are nothing but a facade. You are full of bitterness. I don't know how I could have ever thought that you could be loved."

And with that outburst, I stormed away.

That night, I cried. How I had made an emotional fool of myself for someone so cold-hearted! Was there something fundamentally wrong with me? Was the whole idea of falling in love at first sight nothing but an exaggerated myth?

The next morning, I apologised to Suraj for not heeding

his advice and forcing him to be a part of something he had constantly cautioned me against. He hugged me reassuringly and I knew I was lucky to have him as my best buddy. Then I called up my mother in Benaras. From my voice itself she could make out that something was amiss.

"What is it, Vihaan? What is the matter?" she asked.

"Nothing Ma. I was just missing you and Papa," I told her.

I made a fresh start after that day, trying hard to concentrate on my studies and to erase Zaira from my memory. During the day it was easier because I'd either be in class or with friends. The nights, however, were tougher and I'd end up negotiating between disturbed sleep, and at times, indulging in some natural voyeuristic propensities.

A week went by and I could feel a sense of loss even though I felt more confident with every passing day about coping with it. I tried hard to pump in the optimism that 'my kind of girl' would bump into me soon. And so it turned out to be.

One afternoon, I was woken up from my siesta by the sound of someone knocking on my hostel room door. It was the hostel guard.

"Two girls have come to meet you," he informed me.

Curious, I walked down with him and saw Zaira and Renu waiting for me. I was stunned. Zaira looked uncharacteristically mellowed and somewhat uncertain. I had no clue what had brought them to my hostel, but my insides were shaking with nervousness and anticipation.

"I am sorry for the way I behaved with you that day," Zaira blurted the moment she saw me. "I felt really bad about it later."

I didn't know what to say immediately. I was not expecting an apology. I just stared at Zaira, a serious, thoughtful look on my face.

Chapter One: Delhi, December 1990

"I think I still love you," I muttered, straight-faced, a heartbeat later.

"I don't think I can ever fall in love again . . ." Zaira replied, appearing unmoved.

"Again?"

Zaira half turned to leave without saying anything, before she turned back once again. "I can be a good friend to you though, if that interests you." She seemed to offer an olive branch.

I didn't say anything. Zaira and Renu started walking away.

"So let's be friends," I called out from behind, realising that I needed to take the chance. I walked up to her then and held her hand in mine in a tight clasp. I knew then that I would not leave it, ever.

CHAPTER TWO

New Delhi, February 1991

Life in Hindu college is strange and funny in many ways. One of the incredibly quirky practices which the college students indulge in every Valentine's Day is the worship of an imaginary Damdami Mata.

The Damdami Mata, chosen via voting by the students of the college, is a popular Bollywood actress, usually one who topped the charts the previous year. That year, the chosen Damdami Mata was Kimi Katkar, Bollywood's raunchy sex siren, who had whetted up everybody's fantasies by crooning provocatively to Amitabh Bachchan in the hit song *Jumma Chumma De De* from the film, *Hum*.

As per practice, the oldest tree in the campus, conveniently assumed to be a virgin tree, was decorated with posters of Kimi Katkar. These posters were then garlanded with balloons and water-filled condoms. As part of the ritual, students then gathered around the tree and sang a special *aarti* to appease Damdami Mata. It was believed that performing these rituals would help the boys find a partner and lose their virginity within the next six months.

As I stood at the periphery of the gathering and watched others partake in celebrating the madness, my thoughts, not unexpectedly, were focussed on the girl I would anyway end up thinking about every waking moment and at times, even in slumber: Zaira.

Zaira and I had been spending time with each other quite frequently in the last few weeks, conscious always, of the 'just friends' zone we were expected to be in. Over the course of our conversations, I got acquainted with her background. Zaira's father, Bilal Mohammed Bhat, was a leading carpet dealer in Srinagar, while her mother was British. Her father had fallen in love with her mother while he had been studying business administration in London. The two had gotten married and had moved back to India so that Zaira's father could take over the reigns of the family business. Zaira had grown up in an environment of affluence in their eight-bedroom-bungalow in an upmarket Srinagar locality. They had four cars and three pet dogs. Besides, they also had a house in London.

When I first heard of her affluent upbringing, I felt envious. I mean, my father, a lecturer in BHU, used to go to work in his Bajaj Super scooter. It was only when I was around fifteen that he purchased a four-wheeler, a first for the family—a second-hand Ambassdor. We had hardly travelled to more than half a dozen tourist spots in India. We lived in a modest two-bedroom house and led very simple lives. And there I was with Zaira, a girl who had relatives in London and who had already travelled to at least six other countries on family holidays.

But then, life is a great leveller. The turbulence in the Kashmir valley in the last couple of years had left its impact on Zaira's family as well. Their bungalow had been attacked once

Chapter Two: New Delhi, February 1991

and a part of it damaged by an unruly mob—thankfully, Zaira and her family had not been in Kashmir at that time. The reason for this attack was quite disturbing: Zaira's father had shielded a Hindu friend of his in their bungalow despite warnings from terror groups. The attack was a retaliation.

"My father is quite progressive in his thoughts. He hates terror mongering in the name of religion. Besides, he can do anything for a friend," Zaira told me.

For reasons selfish enough, I somehow felt good when I heard this about Zaira's father. Perhaps he would be broadminded enough to accept me as well when the time came, if it ever did.

In one of our meetings, we went for a long stroll on the empty roads inside the Delhi University Secretariat. I had driven Zaira there on an old Rajdoot bike that I had borrowed from Kundan, a friend of mine. This was our first bike ride together. I wasn't sure whether Zaira had sat on a bike before or not, but I discovered that she had.

"A friend of mine had this Enfield Bullet which actually belonged to his father . . ." she said, looking at the bike wistfully before trailing off. It seemed to me that there was something more to the story, but I didn't feel like pushing her for more details.

That evening, for a change, Zaira was inquisitive about me.

"Well, my father teaches Chemistry in BHU and my mother is a housewife, though she helps poor kids around the neighbourhood by giving them free tuitions. I have led a boring life in an equally boring city where the only hang-outs are religious places."

"Somehow, I've always wanted to go on a boat ride in the Ganges," Zaira said, surprising me. "But I'm sure a boring city is better than a violent city," she continued. "Srinagar has been on the edge for the last three years now. All we get to hear are loudspeakers spewing venom. I wish my city was peaceful like Benaras."

When Zaira said this, I felt her craving to *un*-belong to the land she had grown up in. What I couldn't make out yet were the reasons. Was she impacted in a way she wasn't ready to reveal yet?

***

The second week of February in Delhi often springs up the best weather that you can expect in the city. It's that time of the year when the city usually experiences that last bout of intense cold before the weather starts getting warmer. So, while the biting cold can be discomforting, there is this reassurance that it's the last few days of winter. It actually makes you relish the weather a lot more than you normally would.

As we ambled on the empty streets one February evening, I somehow felt encouraged to hold Zaira's hand. I did it with a great amount of hesitation and was about to pull away, but to my surprise she held mine back firmly. There was a smile on her face, a somewhat intriguing and defiant one which almost made it seem like it was a brave facade.

"Is yours a happy family?" she asked me suddenly, leaving me surprised.

"As happy as a middle class family in India normally is," I replied, still a bit confused.

"Mine isn't." She then confided that her parents weren't getting along well. "They have anyway been drifting apart. But yes, after what has happened in the valley in the last couple of

Chapter Two: New Delhi, February 1991

years, my mom just doesn't want to live there. She wants us to relocate to London."

"And your dad won't do that?"

"He's ready to spend more time in London, but he can't give up his business completely. The stakes are huge for him."

"Hmm . . ." I had often observed that social and political disturbances breed problems in a person's personal space as well. And the probability of these problems really becoming big increases when the people involved in the relationship are more opinionated and selfish. To that extent, I considered myself fortunate to have been brought up in an uneventful place like Benaras by parents who were boring, yes, but unselfish.

Before Zaira could open up further, a police jeep stopped in front of us. Communal clashes had been reported in some parts of the city and as a precaution, the inspector sitting inside told us to return to our hostels immediately. The Babri Masjid dispute in those days would lead to several sporadic communal clashes.

That night, after I dropped Zaira back at her hostel and came back, I grappled with my thoughts. I knew how difficult it had become to prolong this facade of 'friendship'. In the course of hanging out with her, I had begun to discover Zaira. She was a lot different from what I had imagined her to be. She seemed more real, more homely beneath her exotic veil. I craved to be with Zaira all the time. I imagined taking her on a boat ride on the Ganges in Benaras. I wanted to see the bungalow she grew up in. I wanted to meet her parents. I wanted to know everything about her. Everything.

***

When the Damdami Mata Puja concluded on Valentine's Day, there were nearly five hundred students who had assembled around the tree from all over North Campus, resolving to attain their *mannat* very soon. While losing my virginity was just as important for me as it was for them, what was more important for me now, after having met Zaira, was that Zaira, whom I unconditionally loved, love me back.

Therefore, February 14 transformed for me, from Valentine's Day to being the day before Zaira's birthday. And when you love someone, you know the kind of opportunities a birthday provides you with.

So, on the 14th, I bunked my classes and landed outside IP College around noon, carrying a bunch of roses and looking like any other guy on Valentine's Day. I had the guard call Zaira in the hostel, but she wasn't in her room. I tried sending a message for Zaira through students I came across at the gate. But much to my annoyance, there was no sign of Zaira. I had been impatiently walking up and down across the gate, holding those roses, for about two hours and I was beginning to get frantic. What if Zaira had left for her local guardian's house?

Finally, at around two in the afternoon, Zaira walked out, looking annoyed.

"What the hell are you up to, Vihaan? Do you realise how many people you must have asked to call me from inside? Don't create this *tamasha* over here!"

I held the roses in front of Zaira in response, looking into her eyes, willing her to understand the depth of my feelings. Her expression softened as she took the roses.

"Happy Valentine's Day," I whispered.

"To you too . . ." she mumbled.

"Any birthday plans yet?" I asked her.

Chapter Two: New Delhi, February 1991

She shook her head even as I tried hard to conjure up the courage I needed to say what I said next.

"Can I, ahem, can I ask you out on our first official date then, today evening?"

Zaira looked at me, absolutely stunned for a moment, as if her worst fear had come true.

"No," she replied, and turning around she started walking away. I waited for her to turn back. I knew she would, and she did.

***

That evening, I drove Zaira to Priya Cinema in Vasant Vihar for a movie and dinner date. Priya Cinema, in those days, used to be the dream place for a date for most North Campus couples. In the absence of cell phones, GPS navigation, and ATMs, however, this journey across the length of Delhi required quite a bit of tedious planning. I had been hopeful that Zaira would agree to the date. Therefore, apart from borrowing his old Rajdoot bike yet again, I had made Kundan also shell out INR 1500 for the occasion.

As I drove Zaira out that evening, I felt a strange nervousness take hold of me. Going out on a date with Zaira, one of the prettiest girls I had ever met, had seemed unattainable a thing for so long that now that it was actually happening, a worrying sense of responsibility seemed to dawn upon me. I had to make this work.

By the time we reached the Priya Cinema complex after getting lost a couple of times and asking almost half a dozen people for directions, the movie had already begun. We decided, therefore, to settle for a dinner date instead at an Indian restaurant inside the complex itself. I actually preferred that as I was already addicted to our long-winding conversations and I didn't want any interruptions.

As Zaira scanned the menu, every dish which seemed to catch her fancy was non-vegetarian.

"Shall we begin with seekh kebabs and then order mutton curry with fried rice for main course?" she queried excitedly.

"Ah . . . well, Zaira, I am a vegetarian," I told her apologetically.

"Really? That's fine then. We can order a vegetarian meal!" she offered gracefully.

I insisted that Zaira order whatever she wanted, but instead, she went with my choice. I wondered if Zaira's promptness in accommodating my choices was some kind of an acceptance of me.

As we settled over a traditional dinner of naan, daal makhni, and matar paneer, I could see Zaira really enjoy the food.

"You know what," Zaira spoke up a little later, "at home I virtually grew up on a British diet—muesli, oats, lentils, soups, pastas, everything a bit *un*-Indian . . ." and in a somewhat mellowed voice she added, "except for a brief phase when I had learnt to enjoy life uninhibitedly."

For a moment, I wanted to probe Zaira on this brief phase she had just referred to, but I didn't. Strangely, I felt a little insecure. I just wanted the conversation to centre around us. I also realised, yet again, how different our upbringings had been because growing up in Benaras, I hadn't even heard of most of the food items which Zaira had mentioned.

"So why did you finally decide to come out with me on a date?" I asked her, changing the topic.

"I don't know," she smiled. "Perhaps I just want to break

Chapter Two: New Delhi, February 1991

free once again and lead the life that I use to until two years ago . . . a life where there were no restrictions, no security threats, nobody really to watch over me . . ." Zaira trailed off, leaving me uncertain about what to say.

"Listen," she spoke up suddenly, "I hope you are not falling in love with me?!" she asked, looking concerned and at the same time a little confused.

I am in love with you, the words echoed inside my head even as I shook my head, smiling.

It was around eleven by the time we finished our dinner. My plan had been to take Zaira to the coffee shop in Hotel Ashoka, where I would arrange for a cake to be brought in at midnight to usher in her birthday. Then we'd spend hours sitting and chatting until it was time to go back to our hostels. But just before we entered the hotel premises, an idea occurred to me and I stopped the bike barely a hundred metres away from the hotel.

"Are you game for some adventure?" I turned around and asked Zaira, who by now was so sleepy that she had begun to rest her head against my shoulder.

"Like what?"

"Let that be a surprise."

"I-I don't mind I guess . . ."

And so began an adventure I would have never thought myself capable of. I drove Zaira through dark deserted highways, crossing Ghaziabad, Bulandshahar, Khurja, and Aligarh, to bring her to the epitome of love—the Taj Mahal.

I had no clue what kept me going through all those miles in the night. I knew I had become greedy and wanted to make most of the opportunity I had with Zaira. Who knew if I would ever get another chance like this again, to ride through the night like that, as if we were without a care in the world? But what surprised me even more than my own impulsiveness was Zaira's acceptance of my behaviour. She didn't seem particularly worried about where I was taking her. Perhaps the simple fact that she was with me was enough for her.

We reached the Taj at around 6:40 a.m., just as the first rays of the sun touched the monument.

Zaira looked at the monument, dazed. She couldn't make out if it was really the Taj in front of her or if it was all just a bizarre dream.

"I can't believe this," she gushed, and turning around, hugged me tightly. "Thank you for giving me the best experience of my life," she whispered.

It did something to me, that moment. Growing up in Benaras, especially in those days, physical contact between a boy and girl, even if it were as minimal as an innocuous hug, wouldn't come naturally. But it wasn't just about this being the first time a girl had held me like this. There was something in the way she held me that moved me.

I held on to Zaira's hand as she gently drew herself out from the hug. We stood looking at the Taj in awe for nearly a good twenty minutes or so, not saying a word. I guess our thoughts and anxieties for each other, for us, more than made up for the silence. We were definitely not just friends anymore. But neither were we in a position to acknowledge the shift and explore what lay ahead for us.

We checked into a small lodge a little later, pretending to be a couple. We wanted to freshen up, have breakfast, and rest for a couple of hours before heading back to Delhi. But fate had other plans for us. By the time we freshened up and came down to grab a bite, a commotion had broken out in the lobby of the lodge. A group of tourists who had been staying at the lodge, wanted to leave for Delhi, but no taxis or buses were available. Apparently, riots had broken out in a village near Khurja and villagers had blocked the highway. They were pelting stones at any vehicle that dared to ply the roads. And to think of it, we had crossed Khurja barely a few hours ago!

"What a close shave!" Zaira mumbled. "What do we do now?"

"I don't know . . . we might have to stay back for a couple of more hours . . ."

"Here?" Zaira frowned, looking around the lodge. "I just hope the riots stop soon enough and we can travel back later in the day."

I nodded. Deep within, however, I felt a flicker of excitement. Zaira and I could very well end up spending the night together if the situation didn't improve. Stranded as we were in a city of strangers, with the threat of danger lurking right around the corner, the whole situation felt much like what you see in a movie. I wasn't sure if I had been inspired by some movie in undertaking this adventure in the first place, but in a twisted kind of a way, fortune seemed to be favouring the brave!

The first thing we did was to find a pay phone for Zaira to call up Renu at the hostel number. Zaira explained the entire situation to Renu and told her to cook up an excuse in case her parents called from Kashmir. She also gave Renu the number of the lodge we were in.

Zaira remained jittery through the rest of the day, worried that somehow her parents would discover the truth about her whereabouts. Hours passed as we waited for some news about the status of the roads. We went out to a restaurant nearby and had lunch. We walked around the neighbourhood where our lodge was, but Zaira remained distracted and preoccupied. By around six in the evening, it became clear that we wouldn't be able to go back to Delhi as the situation hadn't improved since morning. When we went back to the lodge, Zaira paced up and down the room restlessly.

"Let's go back to the Taj and no, I won't listen to any of your objections," I spoke up suddenly, wanting nothing more than to bring Zaira back from whatever was worrying her so much.

Some twenty minutes later, as we stood in front of the Taj, I held Zaira's hand in mine as she looked at the monument, appearing lost. The moon had risen a while ago and in the pale silver light, the Taj looked more than majestic. It cast a spell over us. I held Zaira's face with both my hands and looked into her eyes. She seemed to be struggling with something, as if stuck in some sort of a cusp between an imperfect past and a tense future. I brought her face close to mine, slowly, and when our faces were a breath away, I kissed her, gently, hesitantly. But Zaira didn't pull back. It was just a brush of our lips, a touch so fleeting that I would have missed it had I not been aware of every single detail of that moment. I deepened the kiss a little, emboldened, and it hit me with a jolt, flooding my mind with sensations, with the smell of Zaira, her warmth, her taste, the shape of her face. Both of us broke away at that very moment, overwhelmed.

To my surprise, I saw tears running down Zaira's cheeks.

"Zaira . . ." I began, concerned. Had the kiss reignited memories that Zaira had been trying hard to forget? Had I misinterpreted everything?

"He was a Kashmiri Pandit, Yash Pandit," she began, staring into her hands. "We were the same age and knew each other from childhood since our parents were friends. He studied in the Tyndale Biscoe School and I went to the adjoining school, Mallinson Girls. By the time we were in the eighth standard, we were the best of friends. We were growing up together, discovering things together and spending all our time with each other. When we kissed each other for the first time, we were just fourteen. We didn't do it out of any sentimentality or because we felt that way for each other. We did it because we wanted to experience what kissing felt like. And who better to experience it with than your best friend . . ."

I felt a surge of envy rush through me as I heard all this. Who was this boy who still held Zaira's heart?

"He proposed to me at the end of our tenth standard exams," she continued, oblivious to the riot of thoughts inside my head. "We used to have this event called the 'Socials' between the boys' and the girls' schools and we would wait for this evening throughout the year. Towards the end of the evening that year, when a good twenty-odd students must have still been there, Yash got down on his knees and proposed to me in front of everybody. I was too overwhelmed and stunned to react. I blushed and actually ran off . . ."

A nostalgic smile surfaced on her face and she brushed away her tears.

"For the next two years, we were a couple and everybody knew about it. We'd move around the city together. Every weekend, Yash would take me on a bike ride all around the Dal Lake. Once, it began to drizzle as we were out on a ride, but that didn't stop us. Nothing did . . . On another occasion, we went on an impromptu trip to Gulmarg with a few other friends. Those two years were the best years of my life. We so young, so full of life . . . in all the blissful moments that we spent with each other, we consciously ignored all that was changing in Srinagar. We were too absorbed in each other to take cognizance of anything else . . . and then one day, without us anticipating it, our lives changed forever . . ." Zaira shuddered.

I could see her expression changing. I could foresee a twist in the tale.

"We had just finished our twelfth standard exams when Yash's father was murdered in broad daylight. Uncle used to head All India Radio Srinagar, and he had been under immense pressure to have the radio channel carry out anti-India propaganda. He withstood the pressure defiantly, but in the end he had to pay with his life."

I froze, trying to visualise whatever Zaira was narrating.

"Things spiralled from there . . . One night, a few weeks after his father's death, some local goons landed up outside Yash's house in the Abi Guzar locality and started hurling abuses at him and his mother, warning him to stay away from *hamare quam ki ladki* (a girl from our community). In no time, Srinagar was an entirely divided city. It was the Kashmiris against the Indians and it goes without saying that all the non-Muslims were considered Indian."

I felt my blood boil at what I was hearing.

"The worst thing was when my dad called me to his room and said he wanted to discuss something. He knew how close I was to Yash and how his father's death had impacted me as well, and yet, he looked straight into my eyes and told me to forget Yash . . ."

"What? But why?!"

"Because Yash was not a Muslim and the people—they wouldn't have let him live there . . . I was shocked that my dad, a man who considered himself a liberal intellectual and a

Chapter Two: New Delhi, February 1991

diehard romantic who had gone against his own family to marry a British woman, was now asking me to break off all ties with Yash simply because he belonged to another religion. I couldn't believe it. I knew there was more to it than what he was letting on. When I finally persuaded him to tell me the truth, he told me that he had been warned that if I continued my relationship with Yash, they would not only destroy his business, but would also kill Yash . . ."

Tears had begun to flow down Zaira's cheeks once again. I wiped them away with my handkerchief, feeling more protective of her at that moment than I had ever felt before.

"Less than a week later, I was packed off to Delhi to do my graduation. Yash and his mom shifted to Jammu to one of their relative's home. We never even got to say goodbye . . ."

I hugged Zaira then. So heart-wrenching was her story that I felt choked even trying to visualise it.

"You haven't been in touch with Yash since then?" I asked, without a clue that the worst was yet to come.

Zaira took a deep breath before answering my question. "About ten months later, Yash came back into my life. He just landed up outside my college one day. We were meeting after such a long time that I had thought I had gotten over him. But no. We realised that our absence from each other's lives had actually made us love each other more. Despite our best efforts to restrict the parameters of our association, we got back into a relationship. Every month, he'd make a trip to Delhi and we would spend a couple of days together. And when we were together, it seemed like there was no tomorrow, no world beyond us. That's how we thirsted for each other.

"But things were just not meant to be permanent between us. My dad somehow got to know about us. He was furious and warned me to end the relationship right away, but Yash and I were too much in love to heed his advice. We continued meeting each other in the months that followed, until one day, just like that, Yash didn't turn up for our monthly meeting. For nearly three months, I heard nothing from him. I went mad with worry. It wasn't like Yash to disappear like this. I contacted some of our common friends and managed to get his mother's phone number from them, but she too, knew nothing about him. She had already gotten in touch with the police, but they weren't helpful at all. It was as if he had vanished into thin air. I turned to my father then and even though he had been against our relationship, Dad tried whatever he could to find out about him. It was only much later that we found out that Yash had gone to Srinagar to get some things back from their abandoned house there. He had taken a bus back to Jammu, but somewhere halfway, he went missing. Nobody knows what happened to him."

Zaira broke down completely as she narrated this last bit. I held her as she wept, supporting her catharsis even as I battled a storm of emotions inside me. I felt more protective towards her, yes, but at the same time I felt like an outsider: she belonged to someone else.

That night in our cramped room, Zaira fell asleep while I lay awake and tried to make sense of my thoughts. It was less than three months since I had first spotted Zaira in the Hindu College fest. Was it some sort of a premonition about there being an unusual story behind the words she had recited that day on the stage that had propelled me to her? Or was there something else that drew me to her? Zaira had not led a normal life. She had seen and been through more than I might ever experience in my entire life. As I grappled to come to terms

Chapter Two: New Delhi, February 1991

with her story, I felt an intense urge to embrace her and nurse her wounds. I wanted to heal her, but I didn't know how to do that. This was the second consecutive night I remained awake until the wee hours of the morning.

Thankfully, the morning brought in some good news. The violence which had broken out the previous day seemed to have settled down and vehicles were back on the highway to Delhi. When we started our drive back, strange as it may sound, neither of us were too happy about it. I guess at times a journey can do strange things to you! Perhaps Zaira was confounded by her sudden change in behaviour towards me. Or maybe she was still reeling from having reopened those old memories the night before, but as we drove back I felt Zaira rest her head on my shoulder, more naturally, more comfortably, and I couldn't help but wonder, could she be falling in love with me too? I doubted it the very next instant. She was still not over Yash and she might never be over him ever.

***

"You didn't tell me anything about yourself," Zaira asked me with a glint in her eyes. We had stopped at a roadside dhaba halfway through our journey and were sipping chai.

"You didn't ask me anything!" I retorted.

"Well, I am asking now . . . any girlfriends I should know about?"

"Nope," I shook my head. "I have never had a girlfriend, not yet. There was one girl I had a mad crush on when I was in the ninth standard. She used to live in the same locality, a few houses away. She was two years older to me . . ."

"Wow! So you're into older girls, huh?"

"You're not older than me!" I shot back, catching her unaware. But Zaira gathered herself and conveniently ignored my comment.

"What happened then, with that girl?"

"Nothing. In Benaras you virtually stalk the girl, try and steal glances, and let her know how you feel, *nazare milana* as you call it. I did it for a good two years . . ."

"And? She responded?"

"She acknowledged me a couple of times and smiled coyly. Then one day she looked terribly irritated when she saw me loafing around her house. The very next day, I was told off by a school senior because his best buddy was seeing the girl."

"And you backed off?" Zaira asked, grinning.

"In Benaras there's not much option. Often, you get beaten up for sending out 'feelers' to someone else's girlfriend. And here I knew I didn't have any chance with the girl," I tried reasoning out.

"And that's all the experience you have of romance? Have you ever kissed a girl? Made out with anyone?"

I struggled for an answer. I was a virgin and consciously so. I wanted to make love only with the girl I was really, really in love with. And now I knew who it would be.

"Shall we leave?" I asked, trying to change the topic.

"Will you take me on a bike ride from Srinagar to Pahalgam?" she asked me suddenly as she got up to leave, surprising me as much as she seemed to have surprised herself with that query.

"Umm, okay. When do you want to make the trip?" I asked her.

"Ah . . . w-w-well . . . forget it," she tried covering up her confusion with a forced smile.

I nodded, deciding to let the matter rest for the time being.

Chapter Two: New Delhi, February 1991

The last leg of our journey was rather strained; more so when Zaira revealed after much prodding that the bike ride between Srinagar and Pahalgam that she had asked me about earlier was something she had originally planned with Yash. It never happened because Yash's father was killed before that and everything just went haywire from thereon.

I struggled hard to keep my emotions in check. Would Zaira ever find it possible to love someone else? Would all her memories always go back to him? How was I ever going to compete with the spectre that was Yash?!

It was well past 4 p.m. by the time I dropped Zaira to her hostel gate. The minute she got down, the security guard at the gate informed her that her parents had dropped in to meet her in the morning.

"Oh God!" Zaira exclaimed, looking pale. "My dad has this habit of not informing me about his Delhi trips and surprising me at times!"

"Where does he stay in Delhi?" I asked, trying to sound calm.

"Usually at the Taj Man Singh Hotel."

"Well, let's go then. The sooner you get there the better."

Zaira nodded, but I could sense that like me, she too did not want to part. I kick-started my bike and pressed the first gear, shoving all other thoughts aside.

"Zaira, can I hug you?"

She nodded. I turned off the bike, got down, and hugged her tight.

CHAPTER THREE

New Delhi, May 1991

The two months that followed our Agra trip were really tough months for both of us. Zaira and I couldn't meet each other much as our final year exams were round the corner. By her own admission, Zaira found herself too distracted and drawn to me. Therefore, she wanted to avoid meeting me too often. As for me, I too, didn't mind meeting her about once in the week because thoughts about her anyway kept me occupied the rest of the time. Besides, I didn't feel as desperate or insecure as I used to before our Agra escapade. Now, even though Zaira's past cast a dark shadow over us, there was this reassurance that my feelings weren't entirely one-sided. Zaira wasn't completely unaffected by me.

On one such occasion when I landed up outside Zaira's hostel, she was about to go meet her parents who had dropped in on a surprise visit. It seemed like an impulsive thought on her part but when she came out to see me, she asked me if I'd like to come along with her. I wasn't really sure, but at the same time I didn't want to let the opportunity go—I was curious about everything related to Zaira. So I tagged along with her in a rented Contessa sent by her father.

Bilal Bhat was a suave, sophisticated, good-looking man in his late forties, with a salt-and-pepper French beard, sharp cold eyes, and an accented English and Urdu diction. One look at him and I immediately felt like a country bumpkin. His wife, Catherine, was gorgeous and seemed to be a simpler human being, not at all as calculative looking as her husband.

As Zaira introduced me to her parents and we exchanged pleasantries, her father asked me what my parents did.

"My dad is a professor in BHU and my mom is a housewife."

"Ah nice! I am sure they lead simpler happier lives than us," he said.

I smiled. "True, life in Benares is simpler. How are things in Kashmir? I understand there have been threats to you and your business . . ."

"Ah these separatists, they are bloody thugs. They are used to fleecing both India and Pakistan. They can swing either way, depending on who gives them a better deal! There was a time when people like Sheikh Muhammad, with whom I was associated quite closely, voiced their opinions vociferously, putting only the larger interest of the people above all else, but look at these separatists now!"

"Kashmir is not a place to live anymore," Catherine added, sounding more hopeless than her husband. "In the twenty years that I have been there I have witnessed the radicalisation first-hand. And mind you, it's downright scary."

"Anyway, there is still hope," countered Bilal, looking at Catherine pointedly. "At least I am confident that the more humane virtues of Sufism will ultimately prevail."

In the hour that I spent with Zaira and her parents, what

struck me was that Zaira's parents were like friends to her. She had her differences with them but at least she could open up to them. In my case, the usual bourgeois distance between my parents and me was virtually impossible to bridge. I could never imagine having political arguments with them or confiding in them about anything.

Zaira was staying back with her parents in the hotel that night. When it was time for me to leave, she came out to the bus stop with me.

"So did you like meeting my parents?" she asked me.

Instead of answering her question, I leaned in and kissed her hard, not unaware of my surroundings but not really caring a whit about it anyway.

"I love you," I told her, looking into her eyes.

Zaira said nothing for a moment, and then, she hugged me before hurrying back inside.

***

It was the second week of May and summer had set in. My exams had just gotten over the previous day while Zaira still had her final paper that day. I felt restless. The fact that Zaira and I had not met for a good sixteen days was driving me insane. My yearning for her was like a constant physical ache in my gut. I wanted to passionately kiss Zaira. I wanted to hold her in my arms and never let her go. Thankfully, we were supposed to meet in the evening after she was done with her exam. Both of us were going away for a week the next day, she to her parents' home in Srinagar, and me to Benares to attend a cousin's wedding. Beyond that lay an uncertain future where our paths would diverge—I wanted to pursue a course in journalism and she wanted to do a Master's degree from JNU. Life as we had known it all these months, would change, and this last evening that we had together seemed burdened already with all our doubts and anxieties. But, wanting to make it a little special, I had borrowed Kundan's bike again and had also asked him for a favour.

When I saw Zaira walk out towards me that evening, I could feel my heart start thumping. I hadn't known I was capable of loving someone this intensely. How could a separation of just sixteen days do this to me? I hugged her hard, smothering her face with kisses and caressing her hair, not caring who saw us.

"How are you?" I mumbled, holding her close.

"Are you all right?" Zaira asked me, looking embarrassed and a bit concerned as well at my behaviour.

I nodded, breaking away from her a little to study her face, wanting to memorise every line, every tiny detail on it.

We spent the evening at the lawns surrounding India Gate, watching the crowd, eating ice-cream, talking, and just savouring each other's company. As the evening shadows lengthened, we couldn't help but return to the topic of our future together.

"Vihaan, we will be fine . . . our bond will remain intact, no matter where we are or how many miles separate us," Zaira told me, holding my hand reassuringly.

I nodded, though not entirely convinced. "Can we do another night out?" I asked her nervously a moment later.

"Agra again?" she teased.

I shook my head. "It's Kundan's birthday tomorrow and a bunch of us have planned a surprise midnight party for him at his house in Malkaganj. I want you to come with me," I blurted out.

"Oh! Well, okay . . . I guess I can come along," Zaira

Chapter Three: New Delhi, May 1991

said, agreeing to my suggestion much more easily than I had anticipated.

When we reached Kundan's house later that evening, I opened the door with the spare set of keys he had given to me when I had first approached him with the plan. Zaira found this surprising.

"Normally one set of keys is with me . . . I come here often," I lied.

When we entered the house it was to find the hall filled with heart-shaped balloons and colourful paper streamers hanging from the walls. Kundan had clearly gone more than a little overboard in trying to give me a good romantic setting.

"Wow! Heart-shaped balloons and all huh? I didn't know boys liked this sort of stuff!" Zaira teased, looking around. "But where is everyone? Where are your friends?" she asked, looking a little confused.

"There's no surprise birthday party . . ."

"Whatttt?" Zaira shrieked. "Then what's all this for?"

"To celebrate us . . . our togetherness," I said, walking up to her and looking passionately into her eyes. I brought my face closer to hers. Zaira didn't move. She didn't pull back. Instead, she surprised me with a gentle kiss on my lips. I shuddered, passion flooding my body. We kissed deeply then, holding each other tight, devouring each other.

I undressed Zaira gently, running my hands all over her face, her body, learning the shape and the curve of her. From her small ears to her delicate feet, every detail was exquisite. I still didn't know if we'd go all the way and make love, not in that moment, but just being able to touch her changed everything for me. I had no clue what was going on in Zaira's mind, she certainly seemed lost somewhere. Her eyes were closed and her breathing was a little erratic. Was this triggering back memories she had been trying hard to supress?

"Zaira . . ." I began, caressing her face.

"Let's do it, Vihaan," she whispered in my ears.

"Are you sure?"

But Zaira didn't answer my question, she just kissed me long and hard, shattering all my restraint.

That night was a night of magic. We made love, we talked, we ate, we made love, and we talked again until we finally fell asleep, draped in each other. How I wish I could have kept those hours frozen somewhere in some deep memory bank. We would have been inseparable ever after then!

I woke up the next morning to the sound of someone sobbing. It was Zaira. She was sitting on the edge of the bed, her eyes all red and swollen.

"Zaira! What happened? Are you okay?" I ran to her.

She just held out the morning newspaper to me and pointed to a small news item on the front page—A Kashmiri Hindu student who had been missing for over a year had been found dead, with grievous injury marks on his body, somewhere midway on the Jammu-Sringar highway. It was Yash. Zaira's Yash!

That morning, when I saw her off at the college hostel before heading to the railway station to leave for Benares, I felt a foreboding sense of loss. Zaira had completely broken down earlier. While I had held her as she wept, trying to support her as much as I could in this grief, I had felt a cold fear grip my heart. Why now? I couldn't help but wonder. Why did the news come in just after we had made love?

Chapter Three: New Delhi, May 1991

Zaira had completely shut herself up and that worried me. All my questions had received monosyllabic replies. A part of me wanted to stay back with Zaira and see her through this, but that wasn't possible. If I skipped my cousin's marriage, my family wouldn't let me live in peace.

The seven days that I spent away from Zaira felt like seven long years. Even as my family busied itself in a million marriage arrangements and ceremonies, my despondency and my aloofness were all too visible. The only contact I had had with Zaira was when one night, about two days after arriving in Benares, I snuck out on my Dad's scooter and travelled a good four kilometres to a telephone booth to make a four-minute-call to Zaira on her landline number.

Thankfully, it was Zaira who answered the call. "I miss you, Vihaan," were her first words. She sounded choked and emotionally distraught.

"I miss you too, Zaira . . . I-I-I can't be without you. I can't wait to see you . . ."

"I need to talk to you about something, Vihaan . . ."

I felt a slight shiver run down my back when she said that. But Zaira refused to tell me over the phone what the matter was. So, since we would both be back in Delhi by the beginning of the coming week, we decided to meet outside her college gate at around eleven on next Wednesday morning. As I kept the phone down, for some unknown, eerie reason, I couldn't shake off the feeling that everything was going to come crumbling down around me. It was like a familiar feeling, only this time it felt more menacing.

That night when I reached home, I was confronted by my parents about my behaviour.

"There's something seriously amiss with you. It's visible to everybody now," Dad said. "What is the matter with you? Are you in some kind of trouble in Delhi?"

"Look at me," Mom said when I didn't answer Dad's question. "What is it, *beta*? What is troubling you?"

"I am in love with a girl, from Kashmir . . . a Muslim girl," I said, staring at my parents defiantly.

My parents didn't say anything to me that night but the tension that my confession created prevailed all the way through the rest of my stay in Benares. We hardly spoke to each other, especially my father and I, lest it result in an awkward situation. I was like an automaton in the days that followed. On the day of my cousin's wedding, as the bride and groom took the *saat pheras* to solemnise the marriage, all I could imagine was Zaira and I doing the same.

When it was time for me to leave a day after the wedding, I could sense my parents wanting to have a conversation about Zaira before I left.

"There's no point arguing with him," Dad told Mom when she tried to bring up the subject again just as I was leaving for the railway station. "He has a tendency to learn things the hard way. Let him do what he wants to."

There was an awkward silence in the room for the next few minutes until Mom took my side, like she invariably did.

"Is there a way I can meet her?" she asked, surprising me.

I nodded and hugged her. At least I had Mom by my side now.

***

I reached Delhi on the morning of 22 May and the moment I got out of the train, dread hit me like a solid brick wall. I can never forget the day or the sense of gloom that seemed to have

Chapter Three: New Delhi, May 1991

gripped everything around. People on the platform seemed to be struck by grief and shock. They were huddled around transistors, listening to the news. And so it was that I discovered that former PM and Leader of Opposition, Rajiv Gandhi, had been killed the previous night in a terror attack in the southern town of Sri Perimbudur.

It was the sort of devastating news that leaves everyone in a pall of gloom for weeks. Considering the former PM's young age and pleasant disposition, it was worse still. I forced myself to snap out from the shock and head directly to IP College.

I reached the college at around noon, an hour late because most buses and autos were off the roads as a sign of mourning. I walked up to the guard and asked him to call Zaira on the hostel phone but he told me that Zaira wasn't there.

"Are you Vihaan Shastri?" he asked me instead, looking me up and down.

I nodded.

"Well, Zaira had come here last evening and left a letter for you. She told me you would come by today morning," he said and handed over an envelope to me.

I found myself shaking as I took the letter. What could be there in the letter which Zaira couldn't have waited till morning to tell me about personally? And where was she? Why wasn't she there to meet me? I opened the envelope, dread gripping my heart.

Vihaan, it hurts me to write this letter, but after thinking a lot about it, I have come to the conclusion that we don't have a future together . . . In the last seven days that you've been away, I realised two things. One, that I love you immensely, and two, that I will probably never be able to get over my past completely.

Every single day that you were away, I missed you terribly. I missed being able to talk to you, to see you . . . but I also couldn't get Yash out of my thoughts. The news of his death on the day we made love completely devastated me. It reminded me of something that happened almost three years ago when Fahad, my cousin from Lahore, had come visiting and the two of us had gone out for lunch in Lal Chowk. That evening when Yash came to pick me up for our regular bike ride around Dal Lake, he was seething with anger. He drove like a maniac, scaring me. I kept asking him what the matter was but he wouldn't tell me. He just kept driving around the lake. People were beginning to look at us suspiciously. Finally, he stopped the bike at an isolated spot near Nishat Bagh and told me that he had seen me have lunch with Fahad. Since he didn't know Fahad was my cousin, he suspected him to be a suitor. That day I saw the possessive side of Yash, something which I hadn't known existed. Even as I explained the situation to Yash, it took a while before he really calmed down. I asked him if he was insecure about me but he shook his head. We stayed there for a little while longer and just as I thought things were returning to normal, Yash said something that left me completely stunned: I don't know why, but I feel I will not live to see the day you don't belong to me.

Those words have haunted me since then. And when I read the news about Yash's death on the morning after you and I had made love, it spooked me. It seemed like Yash's premonition had come true . . . His words ricochet within me day in and day out. They don't let me live . . .

I was stunned with what I was reading, but I forced myself to continue:

Chapter Three: New Delhi, May 1991

I don't want my past and my future to clash and explode upon me. I don't want to be unfair to you. The wounds that I carry, wounds caused by the violence in Kashmir, they may never heal. I want to go far away to escape my demons. Mom has decided to separate from Dad. I am moving to England with her. I will be gone by the time you reach Delhi. I don't have the courage to meet you in person and tell you all this . . . I just couldn't have looked you in the eye . . .

Tears flowed down my cheeks as I felt myself go numb.

For all the beautiful moments that you have given me, all the memories that we made together, I will always be grateful to you. You deserve someone more sorted, someone who is capable of loving you unconditionally . . . Stay happy, Vihaan, and forget me.

I couldn't hold myself from breaking down then. I cried right there outside the hostel gate, oblivious to the stares of the passers-by. The only girl I had truly loved in my life was gone, just like that. The prospect of never seeing her again shook me to my core. There was no email, no phone number, no address I could use to keep in touch with Zaira. She had removed herself from my life without a trace!

A day later, as I watched the images of Rajiv Gandhi being cremated, I couldn't help but feel a chilling sense of personal loss bog me down. As the flames crept up the funeral pyre, they seemed to mark the death of the most beautiful relationship I had experienced in my life.

***

If love can fade, so too can hurt . . .

As days, weeks, months, and years went by, I was to realise that while the hurt and the pain could fade away slowly, the love wouldn't. I loved Zaira more than anybody else could. There was no reason to this love and when there's no reason, love itself becomes the biggest reason to keep that person alive in your memories and thoughts. And so it was with me . . .

I would often imagine Zaira to be around me, sharing happy and sad moments with me. Sometimes, in the most mundane of moments, I would even feel her presence. I knew she would come back into my life one day. I was convinced about it. Karmic connections, after all, never leave you easily.

PART TWO

ZAIRA:
A CHEQUERED LIFE

CHAPTER FOUR

Cancun, Mexico, September 2003

Even though the ocean is calm
Why does an unknown cacophony keep me tense?

Even though there is love around,
Why doesn't the touch make me warm?

Even though there is a crowd everywhere,
Why isn't the one who means the most, seen anywhere?

Even though life seems complete
Why do I feel emptiness creeping in?

Even though I try to hold the memories tight
Why is the sand slipping through my palms?

It has been twelve long years now since I left India, never to return. I had been a wanderer then and I am a wanderer now. When I look back, my life only reminds me of the maxim *Past Imperfect, Future Tense*.

I left India in May 1991, soon after my graduation, when I virtually fled to the UK. Mom had decided to separate from Dad and move back to London—she was anyway making the trip to be with her ailing mother. I decided, at the very last minute, to tag along with her. In my heart of hearts, I wanted to flee the country and never come back. I can't explain what my state of mind at that point was but I have never felt as perplexed about things as I did then.

I had convinced myself into thinking that I had just about managed to move on from my first love, Yash, when I met Vihaan. Something about him, his simplicity, his persistence made me open up to him, I think. When we made love that night in that empty house in Malkagunj, to be honest, it was only because I had persuaded myself to give in. I wanted the intimacy to help me exorcise the memories of Yash. It was a painful yet liberating experience. I felt something unlock within me, as if some part of me that I had kept locked up ever since Yash disappeared, was ready to come out now . . . Once it got over, I heaved a sigh of relief. I was beginning to believe that God had deliberately made Vihaan enter my life. Why else would I end up meeting and making love to a boy from Benaras, whom I had not even been prepared to befriend until just a few months ago?

However, destiny it seems, had other plans for me. When I woke up the next morning and picked up the newspaper from the doorstep, I was confronted with something I wasn't in the least prepared for—they'd found Yash's body on the Jammu-Srinagar highway. Yash was dead. How could that be? How could he die?

I died a hundred deaths that day. I wanted to go to Jammu and see him one last time, but I knew I would not be able to handle that moment. I couldn't bear to see him like that, cold and lifeless. His death would have provided some sort of a closure, I guess, had it not been for the memory of his premonition about not living to see me belong to someone else. I knew then, with Yash's words going round and round in my head, that I wasn't prepared to embrace anybody else. Not for a long time yet.

I realised I couldn't meet Vihaan. I knew he was madly in love with me. I wanted to love him back too, but I just couldn't. I didn't have the courage to face him and tell him that I wasn't prepared for him, for us. And so I flew away to London, leaving only a letter for Vihaan behind.

In London, I tried starting life afresh. I stayed with my maternal relatives for the first few months until Mom found a place for us as her divorce from Dad got finalised. I joined a creative writing course in the University of London. Dad would make a couple of trips a year and stay in a hotel just to spend more time with me. I could see he was trying hard to keep our bond intact even as the distance between us grew. I was also getting news from a school friend back in Srinagar about him getting close to a much younger woman and also beginning to sympathise with the separatists, even though he still publicly abhorred them. I guess Dad was all about dichotomies of various kinds.

One night in 1995, Dad called me, sounding a bit stressed.

"Zaira, I want to tell you something," he said.

"Oh, well, go ahead then . . ."

"I want to start my life afresh. I've decided to marry again."

The girl in question, Noor, was merely three years older to me. She was the sister of one of his business associates. They had met at a wedding where Dad had been mesmerised by her looks. And true to his nature, he chased her in style till she acquiesced.

"I want you to be there for my wedding," he told me.

I couldn't believe him when he said that. I had no intention of attending his marriage and I told him so then and there. Though Dad tried his best to stay in touch with me just like before, I felt increasingly detached from him after this, and more so after his marriage. I tried empathising with his situation. A fresh start with a new partner carries its own challenges. But things kept getting strained between us. What I found increasingly worrying was hearing from family friends back in Kashmir about him attending Hurriyat meetings and supporting the separatists. I tried talking to Dad about the whole issue a couple of times but he was always so evasive that I gave up eventually. This only added to the growing distance between us. In fact, as the years crept by, this distance only increased.

Meanwhile, after my creative writing course got over, I started working for a travel magazine. The assignments required me to travel a fair bit and I ended up going to Australia, New Zealand, and South Africa, covering different stories. The job allowed me to escape all the feelings of hurt and betrayal that life had repeatedly left me with. Mom was aware of my feelings and of my constant need to escape, but we seldom talked. I just didn't have that sort of a connection with her anymore. And what with Dad marrying again, she had her own issues to deal with. I often felt like talking to Dad, but I stopped myself because I didn't want to intrude into his private space anymore. I felt alienated from both of them.

Despite being a voracious traveller, I largely led a reclusive life. I had never had many friends in London. I wasn't into partying or socialising. And with my erratic schedule, it wasn't easy to stay in touch with people. I preferred that. I had also consciously avoided getting into another relationship in all the years since Vihaan. My lifestyle was simple: I'd get to work, write, travel, get back home or into the hotel room early and immerse myself in books or my favourite TV shows. And start again the next morning.

This continued until 1996, when Dad made a sudden trip to London to spend Christmas with me. We went on a long drive to the snowy countryside.

"I want to have a talk with you," Dad told me.

By now I'd begun to find these words from Dad quite amusing.

"Are you divorcing your young wife now?' I asked him, unable to control my laughter.

He shook his head, surprised at my weird sense of humour. "No, but I feel you should settle down . . ."

And a little less than three months later, I met Aziz Hussain at a restaurant in downtown London, on Dad's insistence. The meeting had been mutually arranged by our fathers, eager as they were to see their children 'settled down'.

Aziz was a young and dashing IFS officer, five years older to me. The Indian High Commission in Paris, where he worked in a senior capacity, was his third posting.

I went to meet Aziz, the least concerned about the outcome of our meeting, nonchalant as always. But I found him quite charming. He had done his Masters from the London School of Economics and could talk for hours on almost any subject. He kept me entertained for the hours that we spent together, jumping from topic to topic, sharing anecdotes, asking questions. Besides, our Kashmiri roots gave us more than enough fodder for our conversation.

When I came back home later that evening, I kept mulling about our meeting. Over the next few days, I kept thinking on and off about Aziz. I realised that I wanted to meet him again.

We had exchanged our telephone numbers and Aziz called

me a few days later after returning to Paris. He enquired if there was any likelihood of my work taking me to France in the near future, but I frankly didn't know about that at that point. He called me again two weeks later and we spoke about mundane things—books, movies, work, et al.

Our next meeting happened two months later, in France. I had purposely taken a writing assignment that had me cover the beaches of southern France. I flew in a day in advance to spend some time in Paris before starting the assignment. And to meet Aziz.

"Mind if I join you for this trip?" Aziz asked me when I told him about my assignment over dinner, surprising me.

"Sure!" I replied, thinking he was kidding and laughing it off.

"What? I am serious!"

"Umm . . ."

"You're not a prude or do all Kashmiri women become prudish once they set foot in Europe?"

"Sorry?" I uttered, a bit taken aback.

I found Aziz's words to be chauvinistic, even though I wanted to believe they were unintended. Aziz, on the other hand, was visibly upset. He actually wanted to take this trip with me.

We travelled first to Nice and then to a couple of other beaches nearby. I found Aziz a bit strange, yet fascinating. When he talked he was very articulate and affable, but when he got lost in his thoughts it was very difficult to bring him out of his reverie. At times I thought he was far too well read and erudite for me to understand his moods. But then he would accompany me when I went exploring the beaches and scouted around for interesting angles for my story. We had a decently good time by the end of the trip. In a strange way, I found him nutritious. I felt I could grow and evolve in his company.

We kissed in a beach shack on that trip, after a dinner of oysters and lots of wine. It was my first kiss since that night with Vihaan and I didn't want to go beyond that, not just yet.

When we returned to our respective lives, me to London and Aziz to Paris, we both knew that our relationship had moved a step further. We continued to meet intermittently in the months that followed, whenever our schedules allowed it. And when Aziz proposed to me six months after we first met, I said yes only after about a week's mulling. We got married a few days before Christmas and yes, the marriage was an optimistic escape for me.

The first year was absolute bliss. Aziz's hectic work schedule and frequent travelling meant we got very limited time with each other. But the time that we did spend together was nice. We would spend evenings listening to Mozart or going out to the theatre to catch some play or meet friends. Mostly though, we preferred to stay at home and have a quiet evening together. We made love quite often in those days. Once or twice I tried my hand at cooking and failed quite miserably, much to Aziz's amusement. After that we mostly ate out since we enjoyed experimenting with different cuisines. Aziz took me along on an official visit to Peru and Brazil and we had the time of our lives, gorging on the local cuisine and savouring some of the most gorgeous South American beaches. As the months crept by we sort of settled into a simple, non-demanding routine of sorts that sustained our illusion of a happy marriage.

It was around the time when we were approaching our second marriage anniversary when I realised we were in trouble. Aziz had just been transferred to the Indian High Commission in Nairobi. This was his first posting in Africa and we were both taking our time to adjust to the challenges of the posting. More than anything else it was the cultural change that was proving a little difficult to negotiate.

Aziz was mostly preoccupied with work and I was left alone to settle in and set up our home in Nairobi. Somehow, our physical intimacy grew strained as the days passed. Gone were the evenings of enjoying each other's company. And whenever we made love, it tended to be mechanical on Aziz's part, as though he wasn't really into it. For me, making love was about romance, about gentleness and soft touches, not hurried intrusions in the dark. Things only got worse for us from thereon.

A couple of months after shifting to Nairobi, I started feeling a little unwell. I'd feel weak with occasional bouts of nausea and dizziness. It went on for a couple of days but I didn't feel like telling Aziz about it because I knew he was already stressed with things at work. Instead, I took a home pregnancy test.

It was positive.

***

"Whattt?!" Aziz exclaimed, shocked and stunned when I told him I was pregnant.

"Aren't you happy?" I asked, my earlier excitement unexpectedly trampled.

"Of course not! Why would an accident like this make me happy?" he roared.

"Accident? Our love-making is an accident? I don't understand . . ."

"No, the pregnancy is the accident! Listen Zaira, I don't

believe in bringing kids into the world. I know we should have discussed this before, but . . . but I guess it's too late for a discussion now . . . we'll just have to get rid of it."

Aziz's words shook me. I couldn't believe what I was hearing. Yes, he had always been evasive when it came to any discussion about having kids, but I hadn't been prepared for a shock like that. I had never realised just how vehemently he would reject having a child. I was very keen to have the baby. I wanted to become a mother. I kept trying to convince Aziz otherwise for the next couple of weeks, but he remained just as adamant as before. Then one day, we had a major showdown, a showdown so acrimonious that it resulted in me having stress-induced internal bleeding and finally, a forced medical termination of my pregnancy.

The abortion caused two deaths: that of the baby inside me and of the fragile relationship that Aziz and I had. Our relationship was never the same again. Aziz tried his best to make up for the ugly chapter by being indulgent and attentive. He tried taking more time out for me. He'd persuade me to go for long walks with him, where I'd largely remain silent even as he tried to keep the conversation going. He would cook for me, bring home small gifts for me. But nothing could undo what had happened.

"Are you bored of me?" he asked me one night. "I love you, you know?" he said, holding my face and looking into my eyes.

But I had nothing left to say to him.

***

As the months went by and we kept trying to play the normal husband and wife again, I realised that when you have been deeply hurt by your partner, it impedes physical intimacy. I found myself starting to avoid sex on some pretext or the other. Initially, Aziz showed understanding and patience, but after a certain point he retaliated with rude words and taunts which I found difficult to accept. Soon, there came a time when we spent less and less time with each other. It suited us both. We were able to keep up a facade of peace even as we grappled to restore our inner peace.

In May 2001, Aziz was suddenly transferred from Kenya to Mexico. The thing with these sudden transfers is that they can really unsettle you. In the state of mind that I was in in those months, I wasn't quite prepared to adapt to a new place and new people all over again. Fortunately, right about that same time, I discovered and qualified for a writers' residency program in Canada and managed to escape for two months.

On coming back to Mexico City, I realised that conversations between Aziz and me had gotten reduced to a bare minimum, nothing more than a handful of perfunctory words a day. We'd both remain preoccupied in our own thoughts all day. Aziz had started to bring work home and would work till late. After that, quite often, he would go to sleep in another room in the house we had there. I suspected that he was probably having an affair—maybe someone at work or someone he'd met at one of those innumerable office dinners—but I didn't really have the motivation to investigate.

Two years went by in this manner. Aziz would travel a lot and I would keep seeking distractions—books, movies, music, salsa classes, and at one point in time, even taekwondo sessions—because there was nothing else for me to do. I didn't have a job because I didn't have a work permit.

Somewhere along the way, I quietly started penning down

Chapter Four: Cancun, Mexico, September 2003

a novel. I'd work assiduously during the day and then go for a jog in the evening to the community park. I'd come back home, freshen up and then review whatever I had written that day. This became my routine. Aziz and I were completely indifferent to each other by now. He never asked me about what I did during the day or what it was that I kept working on my laptop in the evenings. We'd often even have our meals separately, in the privacy of our own rooms.

And then one night, in August 2003, Aziz suddenly walked into my room.

"Hi," he said, looking a little uncertain.

"Hi, what's the matter?" I asked.

"I-I somehow feel that we should still try and make it work," Aziz said, walking up to me and holding my hand. "I am travelling to Cancun next month for the WTO. Come along with me, Zaira. After the summit we'll take a few days off and be all by ourselves."

"Oh!" Aziz had caught me by surprise. Honestly, I had stopped thinking about 'us' completely. So when Aziz came up with this suggestion, I didn't know how to respond to it, but somehow I found myself too feeble to oppose the idea.

***

Cancun is a coastal city located at the eastern-most tip of Mexico, bordering the Caribbean Sea. Known for its gorgeous golden beaches, it's a blissful getaway, the perfect place to recharge your batteries.

As I lazed around in our plush hotel suite, I knew I didn't have much to do in Cancun except play the bored housewife of a diplomat until the WTO conference was done and Aziz was free.

That morning, the second day of our being in Cancun, I went down for a leisurely swim in the turquoise waters of the hotel pool. After completing a few laps, as I rested myself in one corner of the pool, I suddenly became aware of a man seated at a poolside table close by, who seemed to be watching me rather intently. He appeared to be of Asian origin, but since he was wearing dark glasses and was sitting in the shade, I couldn't quite make out his features. The moment he saw me look at him, he pretended to read a magazine. I found it a bit strange but I decided to ignore the man and continued to swim. Every time I looked around though, I knew he was watching me. I found it surprising that of all the places in the world, I should come across a bikini gazer at this plush resort in the middle of Cancun!

Half an hour later, as I sat with a cup of coffee at the hotel restaurant, I saw this stranger seated at a table just a few metres away from me. He was fiddling with his cell phone distractedly and was sitting with his side profile visible partially to me. I was conscious now. Was I being followed? Or did I know this man from somewhere? When he saw me staring at him, the man got up hurriedly. He put some money on the table for the cup of coffee he hadn't even touched, and disappeared, making it more obvious now that I was being stalked.

Ten minutes later, when I entered the lift to go to my seventeenth-floor-suite, he was there inside the lift. He seemed to be waiting for me. Ignoring the other person, an old lady, in the lift, I lashed out at him.

"Why are you following me?" I demanded.

But the man didn't answer my question; instead, he moved right up to me, planted an impulsive kiss on my forehead, and whispered my name, his voice shaking. Even as the first flickers of recognition hit me, he removed his dark glasses. I couldn't believe my eyes. I couldn't believe it was him. After all these years, the boy I had so abruptly escaped from in 1991 when I had fled from Delhi, the boy who had loved me so much, he had resurfaced in my life, in Cancun, of all places.

I hugged him tightly, old memories rushing back. We didn't exchange a word. The old lady stepped out at the tenth floor and we made the tenth to seventeenth floor journey twice over, just holding on to each other.

We went back to the coffee shop to sit down to talk. Vihaan told me then that he was covering the WTO from the perspective of the Indian delegation at the conference. He explained that he was the top columnist at a leading newspaper back in India. Besides, he had strong political leanings now and was on the cusp of launching himself full-time into politics. He had spotted me the previous day itself, he said, but he just couldn't believe that I could be in Cancun. He'd decided to keep a close watch on me to make sure it was actually me.

"Well, I guess when you're destined to meet a second time, it just happens . . ." I ruminated.

"What brings you here?" he asked.

"I am here with my husband. He's with the Indian consulate in Mexico," I told him.

As we sipped our hibiscus tea, Vihaan looked lost and shaken, perhaps he was remembering some of our moments together all those years ago. I too, felt a little lost, but my now permanent stoicism effectively concealed my true emotions.

We spoke about random things for a while, and then he asked me what he must have been waiting for years to ask.

"Why did you leave me, Zaira? Why? I kept waiting . . ."

"I have been trying to escape myself all my life," I said.

"But why?"

"I wish I had the answer to that, Vihaan . . ."

An awkward silence between us followed.

"Tell me about your life," I asked him finally.

For a moment Vihaan seemed to wonder about what he should say. "Well . . . my story has always been the same, of having a few things I could call my own and wanting to acquire a lot more."

I learnt then that like me, Vihaan had been married for five years now. They'd met through common friends, dated for a while and then, they had had to tie the knot somewhat hastily when his wife's father, who was on his death-bed, insisted on seeing them married. Vihaan's wife, Ritu, was a financial analyst with a venture capital fund and travelled extensively for work. They had a three-year-old daughter, Tia, who was largely looked after by a nanny. They all lived in Mumbai.

"How did the Mumbai shift happen?"

"Well, in a way I was forced into it. Ritu got a very promising assignment for which she had to relocate to Mumbai. She was hell bent on moving, despite knowing that my political aspirations would be better nurtured in Delhi. I am too attached to Tia, and so is she to me, to have stayed back in Delhi. So I shifted to Mumbai in spite of not wanting to. It's tough. I end up making a trip to Delhi every 10-12 days or so."

I could sense a tinge of disappointment in the way Vihaan spoke about Ritu. But I didn't want to read much into it. Most marriages have issues. Some couples try to play down the differences, while others play them up, depending upon how they see their future.

At this point, Vihaan's colleague rushed in and broke up our conversation.

Chapter Four: Cancun, Mexico, September 2003

"Vihaan, here you are! I've been looking all over for you, man! The Indian Commerce Secretary is holding a press briefing. We need you there."

After Vihaan left, extracting a promise of at least one dinner together before he left Cancun, I found myself retreating into a reverie of memories. There were only two men that I had ever really loved in my life—Yash and Vihaan. Yash was dead. And I had left Vihaan behind. But did I really need to let go of Vihaan in that summer of 1991? What if I had stayed with Vihaan? Would we have made it through together? Or would he have left me later? After all, I know it better than anybody else how difficult I can be.

Thoughts of Vihaan kept floating in and out of my mind for the next few hours. I made very determined attempts to get back to my writing. I was left with just the last two chapters of my book. An Indian publisher had already shown interest in publishing my book after I had sent them some sample chapters. Needless to say, however, I was too distracted to be able to concentrate on my writing that day. I felt an unusual anxiety to see Vihaan again.

That evening, as I joined Aziz at the customary official WTO dinner, my eyes kept scanning the crowd in the hall. There were more than a thousand guests around and yet, my eyes were searching only for Vihaan. Aziz, as usual, had official courtesies to take care of, and he left me alone and somewhat abandoned. So I worked my way through the hall and went over to the poolside. But Vihaan wasn't there. I walked to the bar and took a good look at the men sitting there. Vihaan wasn't one of them.

I was about to turn away when I spotted him sitting at one of the raised bar stools at the far end, with the same colleague who had called him away in the afternoon. I was in two minds about what to do—should I intrude or just let go? I turned away, deciding against walking in on what looked like a serious discussion between them.

"Zaira!"

I turned around. Vihaan had spotted me and was walking towards me.

"What a pleasant surprise!" he beamed.

"Y-y-yeah . . ." I muttered nervously.

***

An hour later we were dancing together. What had started off casually, like two partygoers taking to the dance floor and simply enjoying the music, had graduated into a more intimate waltz with both of us dancing really close, holding each other. I leaned into Vihaan, my head on his shoulder, breathing in the smell of his cologne. I wanted this moment to freeze. Was I getting greedy?

I could sense confusion engulf us. I consciously drew myself back a bit. Neither of us was sure what we were getting into. Was our bumping into each other pre-destined, like almost everything else in life appeared to be?

"Zaira!" called a voice from a distance.

It was Aziz. He looked sloshed and also quite surprised to see me dancing with a stranger. We walked over to Aziz, a little awkward.

"Aziz," I began, "umm . . . this is Vihaan, an old friend from college. We just bumped into each other here in the hotel earlier today."

"Ugh," Aziz grunted in response, completely ignoring

Chapter Four: Cancun, Mexico, September 2003

Vihaan. "I've been looking for you. Your cell phone is also not reachable."

"Oh . . . umm . . . should we have dinner then?" I asked him.

"I've had mine. Let's go back now," he said rather indifferently, still not acknowledging Vihaan.

I looked at Vihaan helplessly. "Fine . . . Let's go then," I said, not knowing what else to do. I left with Aziz, leaving Vihaan looking uncomfortable at the edge of the dance floor.

That night, as we lay on the bed, the distance between Aziz and me seemed greater than ever before.

"You told me you studied in a girl's college, right?" Aziz asked me suddenly.

I nodded.

"Then how come this Vihaan chap is your college friend?"

"Well, he obviously wasn't in my college but he's a friend from my college days."

"Hmm." Aziz turned to the other side and slept off.

Aziz had never really bothered about who I spoke to or who I was friends with. Why then, had he questioned me about Vihaan? Was it some kind of a spouse's intuition that had made him inquisitive?

***

Next morning, I sat in my room working on my laptop. Aziz had already left for the conference and I liked the solitude. I wanted to be left alone. I knew I was emotionally fragile and I didn't want to be led into a situation where I would keep thinking about and missing a man who was not meant to be mine. Vihaan and I hadn't gotten around to exchanging our phone numbers the night before. So there was a very good possibility of us not bumping into each other again.

Just then, the doorbell rang, surprising me. I wasn't expecting anyone and housekeeping had already come in and gone. I got up and opened the door, unsuspectingly, only to be shocked. It was Vihaan, looking shaken and nervous.

He hugged me tightly before I could even say a word. "I missed you," he muttered.

"Come inside, Vihaan." I broke away from his embrace and ushered him in.

As we sipped coffee a little later, our conversation remained sparse—Vihaan seemed uncertain about what to say and I didn't quite know what to make of him being in my room.

"You know what," Vihaan began, putting his coffee cup down and fidgeting, "I, I didn't know if at all we'd meet again. So, ugh, I guess the eternal romantic in me just wanted to see you again and steal as much time with you as I could," he tried explaining his indiscretion.

I stared at the man sitting in front of me. In as much as I had tried to hold my emotions back and keep myself closed off, my heart echoed Vihaan's words. I wanted to be a thief, just like him, and steal my moments of temporary joy.

"But what happens to your assignment here?" I asked him.

"Don't worry. I have a competent junior colleague. He will cover for me today."

Vihaan was just as mad and obsessive as he had been thirteen years ago when we had first met. And I loved him for this.

In an hour's time, we were meandering inside a museum that housed Mayan relics. In fact, Mayan relics were an important tourist attraction in Cancun and their presence could be seen in

Chapter Four: Cancun, Mexico, September 2003

almost the entire city. For me, the museum felt slightly eerie. I had always felt that being in any place that lives under the shadow of its glorious past can be a mildly haunting experience. It makes you want to imagine the place in all its ancient splendour. I could, perhaps, say the same thing about Kashmir and also about my own self. Both Kashmir and I had seen our best days in the past; our present existence was just about bearable.

These somewhat melancholic thoughts had me unconsciously reach out and hold Vihaan's hand for a moment, until I realised what I had done and pulled my hand back. The next moment Vihaan held my hand, clasping it hard. I didn't pull back this time.

Dusk found Vihaan and me at one of the most gorgeous places in Cancun: Playa Tortugas, or the Turtle Beach. Our hands were still clasped in each other's. Our conversation throughout the evening had been minimal. What does one talk about anyway in a situation like the one we were in? Neither could we dwell on the disturbed, muddy waters of the past, nor could we make any plans about our uncertain future. Simply savouring each other's company in the limited time we had together seemed like the best option we had. And we were happy, the two of us, having each other by our sides. We didn't want words to disrupt the serenity we felt in each other's presence.

When the last rays of the sun faded away, leaving behind a brilliantly red sky, we kissed each other. It seemed to be the most natural thing to do.

As it grew dark and we sat watching the ocean, I could feel a strange forlornness grip me. I guess I was already missing Vihaan. I didn't want him to go.

"Shall we leave?" he asked a little later, dispelling the long spell of silence.

I held him tightly for a minute and then we left.

That night as I lay alone in my hotel room—Aziz had gone to attend an official dinner—I missed Vihaan terribly. His re-entry into my life and the time we had spent together in the last two days had been a revelation for me. I realised that I was just too detached from Aziz, from the world we cohabited, and that holding on to it didn't seem enticing at all. I wanted to let go of it all. But did Vihaan miss me as much as I was missing him at that moment? He still had feelings for me, yes, but I couldn't figure out if he was as lonely as I was. If he needed companionship and love as I did . . . I tossed and turned through the rest of the night but the answers eluded me.

***

It was the last day of the WTO summit. The session would end a bit early today, at around 5 p.m. Vihaan and I, however, were not at the conference venue. We were not anywhere close to my hotel either. Instead, we were in Vihaan's hotel room, a good half an hour away.

"After you left, Zaira, I just drifted through life and people. I never really fell in love with anyone. Women came and went, but no one mattered. I got married because that seemed like the normal thing to do," Vihaan recalled, sounding resigned. We were sitting next to each other on a sofa in his room, holding hands and sipping red wine. "Now at this stage, instead of even worrying about my personal life, all my focus is on my professional goals. I need to make my transition into politics soon . . . it is the only thing that motivates me now . . . and of course, Tia."

Chapter Four: Cancun, Mexico, September 2003

"Do you love your wife?" I asked him tentatively a moment later, not sure if I should have.

Vihaan looked lost, almost as if he were struggling to find an answer. "I'll have to think about this," was all he could finally manage.

His answer left me confounded and disturbed.

I realised Vihaan's glass was empty and took it from him to refill it. But he held my hand and put the glass back. Then pulling me to him, he held my face in his hands and kissed me. For the next few minutes it felt as if the world outside had disappeared and it was only us there as we kissed. In as much as we were tempted to go beyond the kiss, neither of us really wanted to risk the complications that would inevitably follow.

Vihaan had to attend the closing press conference at the summit and then immediately rush to the airport. We parted with a hug, a hug so intense that it would see me through the infinite separation before, and if it all, we met again.

Hours later as I lay in bed mulling over the unexpected happenings of the last two days, Aziz walked in looking unusually relaxed and a bit drunk, now that the summit was over. He was, in fact, humming an old romantic number. He walked straight to the bed and sat down beside me, a mischievous glint in his eyes.

"Let's do it," he whispered, leering.

These sudden, impromptu sexual demands had always freaked me out. I guess for men it's purely a matter of satisfying a basic need. For me, it was an emotion and a feeling, a lot more than a mere bodily need. It had been months since we had last had sex and it was natural for me to crave for physical intimacy. Yet I couldn't just give in instantly to the whims and fancies of my partner. It wasn't a switch that one could just turn on and off. I longed for a simple, basic touch from Aziz, holding hands, a kiss on the forehead, a hug, anything. But we were too estranged for such gestures.

Nonetheless, I gave in that night. I didn't want Aziz to go back to Mexico City and tell me that my indifference had spoilt our 'holiday trip'. The difference this time was that even as Aziz made love to me, it was not him but thoughts of Vihaan that occupied my psyche. It was Vihaan I imagined making love to me. I hated myself for doing this but I just couldn't stop it.

The moment it was over and Aziz stepped into the bathroom, I turned away and checked my phone—there'd been a message alert sometime back.

The message was from Vihaan. He'd sent it just twelve minutes ago: "Never expected we'd meet again like this. Thanks for being a part of me. The flight is about to take off and I'm feeling as insecure as I did when I dropped you the last time at your hostel twelve years ago. I love you. Bye."

I felt goosebumps on my arms as I read and re-read the message. I immediately called Vihaan, hoping his flight wouldn't have taken off and I could tell him how I felt. But it had.

Feeling suffocated inside the room, I wrapped a sheet around myself and stepped out into the balcony. There I was, naked, but for that sheet, just having had sex with my husband, and it was Vihaan that I missed, Vihaan that I needed. Vihaan had messaged me about his feelings. I wished there was a way he could know mine: that I felt as depressed and vulnerable as I had twelve years ago when I had abruptly taken off for London with Mom, that I would have given anything to have him stand beside me on that hotel balcony in the balmy night air. I wanted to meet Vihaan. I needed to see him again, and for some inexplicable reason I had an intuition that this time the wait wasn't going to be too long.

CHAPTER FIVE

Cancun–Mumbai, 2003–2004

In the months that followed Cancun, Aziz and I continued living together, our detachment from each other only increasing with every passing day. I missed Vihaan several times a day. I yearned to talk to him but I consciously combated my urge. I was holding myself back. I knew Vihaan was an emotional fool when it came to me and I didn't want to be the cause of any more problems in his marriage than were already there. I had been selfish in leaving him abruptly all those years back; I didn't want to be selfish again by re-entering his life at my convenience. Hence, despite my own weakness for him, I felt that not communicating with him at all was perhaps the best thing to do. I had received a couple of emails from him, asking how I was, but I didn't reply to any of them, behaving against my very nature.

But of the many personality traits I possessed, fickleness is one. My first novel, which I finished a little after I came back from Cancun, was now ready for release. My publisher, who was based in India, had suggested a three-city launch tour—Mumbai, Kolkata, and Delhi. The whole idea excited me. I would be a published author now, a feat that was looked at with huge amounts of respect in those days when not everybody could get published as an author. Moreover, I had been away from India for nearly twelve years now. I wanted to go back to Kashmir and meet my father and his new family. I wanted to be brave enough to see him living with strangers as his family. But to be really honest, it was the thought of meeting Vihaan again, with a legitimate excuse in hand, that excited me the most. So, giving in to my fickle heart and with a good degree of tentativeness, I got down to writing an email to Vihaan:

I will be in your city on 16 Jan. My first book, 'Interrupted Love', releases that day. I will be happy if you come . . .

***

"How many days are you going to be away?" Aziz asked me at the dinner table a day later when I told him about my India plan. He sounded impersonal, almost like an employer responding to a leave application by an employee.

"I am not sure. It could be a few weeks or a few months, depending upon how I take to India. I haven't been back in about twelve years after all . . ."

"Hmm," he mulled over it for a moment. "Okay."

And just like that, my leave was sanctioned. I went into a tizzy of activity in the week that I had before I left for India—packing, organising things, coordinating with my publisher, and swinging between nervousness and excitement.

When Aziz dropped me to the airport on the day of my departure, he didn't show any signs that he'd miss me in the coming weeks. We didn't bother to hug or kiss either, not even perfunctorily.

"Take care," he said, "and be in touch."

I nodded, and opening the car door got out as quickly as I could. I couldn't wait to get away. The moment my flight took off, I felt extricated from an onerous bondage.

***

On 16 January 2004, as I walked into Taj Land's End Hotel in Mumbai where my publisher had organised the book launch, I felt a gamut of emotions bubble up inside me. I couldn't quite believe that I was actually going to release my own book. After the string of failures in my personal life, some destined and some not, it was like a boost to my sense of self. It gave me a sense of purpose and direction. But more than anything else, it was the possibility of seeing Vihaan—even though he had not replied to my email—that had me feeling edgy. In the crowd of about 150-odd people that had gathered in the hall, it was his presence that I was seeking and his absence made me feel acutely lonely. The only familiar face in the audience was that of my college friend, Renu, seated in the front row. Renu worked with a top bank in the city in a senior position and lived alone in a pretty little apartment in Khar. In fact, I was putting up with her.

When my publisher quietly indicated to me that it was time for the book to be unveiled, I went up to the stage with Sunaina Bose, an upcoming director of offbeat films. I had written to Sunaina sometime back, requesting her to do the honours. It was kind of her to have accepted my invitation, considering she did not know me at all.

As Sunaina and I unwrapped the book, cameras flashed at me and I put forth my best smile, even if it was rather belaboured and strained. I felt disappointed that Vihaan hadn't made it to such an important moment in my life. Then Sunaina engaged me in a discussion on the book. Steeling myself, I launched myself entirely into it, reading out excerpts from the book and talking about the journey I undertook while writing it.

As I read one excerpt towards the end of the event, I looked up at the audience for a split second and saw him, seated somewhere towards the back. He smiled when he saw me spot him in the crowd. My confidence shot up immediately and I felt reassured. Even as I finished reading out the words on the page in front of me, I was surprised by the effect Vihaan's mere presence seemed to command upon me.

I look into the mirror
And I see a face which looks so dear
Eyes which are moist
Yet so clear
Lips though they wear a smile
Yet not real
A voice from within
Which I always hear
It gives me a pain which is sweet
Yet I fear
A void which is always there
Hope someday it is filled with love and care.

I closed the book and looked up. It was now time for a question-and-answer session with the audience.

"If she knew it was a pattern she had to change, why couldn't she?" asked the familiar guest.

"Well, she was lazy. She waited for her lover to pull her out of this pattern," I responded, thinking largely about my novel but not unaware that my life could well follow fiction.

That night, Renu, Vihaan, and I had dinner at a rooftop restaurant on Linking Road in Bandra. The sea breeze blowing across made the experience simply ethereal. All throughout the meal, Renu could probably feel that Vihaan and I needed to talk alone because the minute we were all done, she excused herself and left, pleading tiredness and a long day at work as excuses.

Vihaan took me out on a drive after that. I was quite mesmerised by the city's glitter and its throbbing pulse. For someone who had only been to Mumbai once before as a kid, I had always had rather romantic notions about the city. I had never imagined that my tryst with Mumbai would eventually be with Vihaan by my side, our old association tossed into an uncanny, new equation now. No wonder the city and what it had in store for me seemed tantalisingly intriguing.

We went to Juhu beach and walked along the sea, letting the water rush and swirl around our feet. Vihaan tried to hold my hand once but I pulled it away, feeling a little conscious and somewhat guilty too. Throughout the evening there had been a distinct undercurrent of tension between the two of us, but for some reason neither of us had broached it yet. I knew Vihaan would want answers for my silence after Cancun, but so far, neither had he asked me anything nor did I volunteer any information. I guess he had given up on some of my idiosyncrasies and was happier ignoring them. But as time trickled by and Vihaan continued to be silent, I couldn't hold myself back anymore.

"Vihaan..."

"Hmm?"

"Are you really not angry with me?"

"Angry? For what?" he asked, turning to look at me with a puzzled smile on his face.

"Ugh... I didn't respond to your mails."

"Ah!" Vihaan nodded. "Well you were just being yourself... this isn't my first experience of your silence." He smiled wryly and held my hand reassuringly.

I didn't say anything, realising that Vihaan probably knew me a lot better than what I had expected.

"Where's your wife?" I asked him a little later when I suddenly noticed that it was around midnight.

For a moment he looked unsure, but then he smiled. "Come, I'll make you meet her."

"Now?!"

Vihaan just nodded and started walking back towards the car.

"Isn't this a very odd time to meet your wife?" I asked, following him. His behaviour was a bit strange. And to be honest, I didn't really want to meet his wife.

"Don't worry. Just relax," was all he said, starting the car.

We drove for a few minutes until we reached his apartment complex in Versova. As Vihaan unlocked the door of his twenty-second-floor apartment and led me in, I realised to my shock that the house was empty.

"What's this Vihaan? You lied to me?!" I asked him, feeling betrayed.

"Well, if I had told you the truth you wouldn't have come, would you?"

When I didn't say anything, he opened the glass doors

which led to the balcony and stepped outside, gesturing to me to follow. A bird's eye view of the glittering city awaited.

"I really wanted to spend some moments alone with you, here, in my favourite spot in the city," he said, looking outside. "But as usual I had to steal those moments."

I walked up to Vihaan and hugged him. I couldn't stop myself.

"Where's your family?" I asked him. I had noticed one wall of the living room done up entirely with a collection of family pictures. There were a couple of photographs of Tia, Vihaan's three-year-old daughter. One of the photographs was of Vihaan and Ritu, looking perfectly happy together. I had looked away.

"Well, Ritu is on a two week-long official trip to San Francisco where her company's headquarters are. She keeps travelling every quarter."

"And Tia?"

"She's with Ritu's sister's family. They stay nearby. Since Tia is close to her cousin, I often send her there."

"You should have told me, Vihaan, that they are not there. I-I-I shouldn't be here . . ."

***

An hour later, we sat in the dimly-lit living room, talking intermittently. In the silence that punctuated our conversation, I sensed that Vihaan was perhaps ready to bare his heart and he did.

"I lead an unfulfilled life," he said. "I guess Ritu and I are together not because we really want to be together, but simply because a lot is at stake for both of us professionally. And neither of us wants to upset this arrangement, whatever it is, at this point."

The word 'arrangement' struck me. I too, was grappling with an arrangement which was disguised as marriage. Did all marriages eventually become arrangements?

"But what exactly is the problem between the two of you?" I asked him.

"Ritu and I are two very different people. Our priorities in life are different. She can't relate to my pursuits and I can't relate to her ambitions. She went back to her job when Tia was barely three months old, leaving her with an irresponsible nanny whom I couldn't stand. And last year when she got a transfer to Mumbai, she didn't once consider whether it would suit me or not, even though she knew I aim to pursue a career in politics."

I could see emotions getting the better of Vihaan as he went on.

"You know Zaira, in today's world, it's men who are the weaker sex. Look at what Ritu did. She did not consider it important to be sensitive to my choices because she knew I would be the one to budge in the end. And you know what gave her that confidence? It was the simple fact that I love Tia too much to be away from her. It was emotional blackmail, every which way you look at it."

"Where do you see it heading?" I asked him, trying to comprehend his situation.

"Well, I am at the brink of a big, possibly life-altering change," he said, almost sounding prophetic.

"And does the prospect of such a huge alteration ever worry you?" I asked. I knew he was a fiery Right Wing ideologue whose articles created a lot of buzz and traction for the ruling party. He was also very likely to contest for a Lok Sabha seat in the upcoming elections.

"It does . . ."

Both of us felt silent then. I rested my head on Vihaan's shoulder and wondered if, in the life-altering changes he was anticipating, there was a place for me or not. Would I ever become a more permanent part of his world? Or would we always flit in and out of each other's life?

I must have been exceptionally weary for I have no idea when I dozed off on Vihaan's shoulders. When I opened my eyes hours later, I found myself on a bed, with Vihaan seated on a chair close to me, reading the newspaper, a tray with two cups and a teapot on the table next to him.

For a moment I felt confused and shocked. I had spent the night in Vihaan's house, in the absence of his wife. I had no right to be there. But what about Vihaan's behaviour? I reasoned with my own self. No sensitive man would bring an ex-lover back to his empty home and then have her sleep over, would he? I was an outsider, intruding into the innermost part of Vihaan's world. Was I really an outsider though? In an official sense, yes. But then Vihaan and I had lived in each other's hearts and minds for thirteen years now. We were far too entangled to be considered outsiders in the literal sense.

"All well?" Vihaan asked me, breaking into my thoughts as though sensing the turmoil inside me.

I nodded.

"You don't feel this is odd, me waking up here, in your house like this?" I asked him straightaway.

Vihaan shook his head and turned to pour out the tea.

"Have you had an affair before, outside your marriage?" I probed him further.

"Not yet," he said, "but I've gone out a couple of times with someone special."

"Really? Who?"

"Yeah, with my ex-girlfriend, in Cancun."

I couldn't help laughing. Maybe this was how it was meant to be, us snatching small moments of joy in the middle of our complicated realities.

"Make sure you don't have an affair with your ex," I cautioned him.

"I am not the 'affair' types. I end up falling in love," he said somewhat ominously.

As I sipped the tea, I realised it was Saturday morning. I was to fly out of Mumbai on Monday morning to continue with the remaining book launch events. After that, I would travel to Kashmir for a few days. I had two days to do as I wanted and all that my heart wanted was to live through these two days with Vihaan as if there was no tomorrow. After a quick breakfast, therefore, Vihaan and I headed out on an impromptu trip to Lonavala.

"Vihaan, are you sure this won't impact your work? I mean elections are round the corner . . . You might be called in for a TV debate or something," I checked with him for the hundredth time.

"When you're around, nothing else is more important," he declared indulgently.

But there was something else that had me worried. Vihaan wasn't an unknown entity anymore. A lot of people knew him. Being seen with a mysterious woman would not do him any good, especially with the elections coming up. But when I said as much to Vihaan, he simply brought out a hat and a pair of oversized dark glasses and put them on. I burst out laughing.

He could have easily passed off as someone else. Vihaan was as crazy, obsessive, and mad as ever. He had not changed one bit, and I loved him for that.

Three hours later, we sat at one of Lonavala's highest rooftop cafes. We almost seemed to be floating in the middle of clouds. It was a liberating feeling to be so far away from the mad rush of the city and the material demands of the world below us.

"Why do you want to be in politics?" I asked Vihaan over coffee. "It's going to take all your peace away." When I said that, I realised I felt protective towards Vihaan like a spouse would.

"In a democracy, politicians are the only people who can actually bring change. The others—bureaucrats, journalists, and the common people, they can only take that change forward, they cannot really initiate the change."

"And what change is it that you aspire to bring in the country?"

"So many of them, Zaira!" Vihaan laughed. "For instance, I want to bring an anti-begging law into force that makes begging a crime. The prevalence of begging, besides it being a cover up for child trafficking, lowers the self-esteem of a society. Of course, there has to be a plan to rehabilitate all those who engage in begging before we make it illegal. It's a structural change that has to be worked out. I also think that our idea of Independence Day needs to change. From celebrating our achieving freedom from British rule, we need to celebrate our five thousand-year-old civilization. Right now, the way we observe Independence Day restricts the history of our great land . . ."

Vihaan spoke passionately about his political vision for a good half hour, elaborating on his plans and his ideas. I was convinced by the end of it, that he wasn't meandering in life, he was on a mission. But to be blatantly honest, I also felt a tinge of disappointment as he spelled out his plans, for I didn't really see any place for me in his life. He may have been trapped in an unhappy marriage, but it appeared to me that Vihaan's responsibilities as a father and his political aspirations were sufficient compensation for him to ignore the inadequacies in his marriage. Then again, I couldn't fault him for not factoring me into his plans because how could he have ever accounted for us meeting again like we did in Cancun? Maybe I was just a convenient distraction for him at the moment, or an old infatuation that he was reliving, but I couldn't ask him for answers.

A little later, the conversation, quite expectedly, drifted to my father's active role in Kashmir politics. My liberal, non-religious father was now a Hurriyat Conference leader in the valley, one of the soft separatists.

"Isn't it surprising how people change over time? I mean, I still remember meeting Uncle at Taj Man Singh and how he had scoffed at the separatists. Who would have thought he'd become one himself . . ." Vihaan wondered.

"Yeah, well . . . Dad has not been the same person after his second marriage," I told Vihaan. Deep inside, I was disappointed with Dad. How could a man who had been a staunch upholder of the liberal spirit for all his life suddenly shift in his political stand so radically?

Vihaan then changed the topic and started talking about his daughter, Tia. I could see that he was an extremely involved father.

"I used to change her diapers, feed her, and take care of her most of the time. In fact whenever Tia is unwell, I just leave everything and stay with her. The first time she laughed, Zaira, you cannot imagine what it did to me . . . I fall in love with Tia every day . . ."

As Vihaan spoke, I felt envious of him having a child. I felt an anger sweep through me that it was Ritu who shared this life with Vihaan, not me. What did she have in her to deserve Vihaan?

I told Vihaan about my pregnancy and how that had irreparably damaged the relationship between Aziz and me.

"You'll make a great mother someday, Zaira," Vihaan said, hugging me.

For a moment, I wished I could have Vihaan's child. But the very next second, I rebuked myself for the indiscretion of my thoughts. I couldn't be thinking like that.

By the time it was dark, it became quite cold and the hotel staff lit a bonfire for us. As we sat there sipping wine and warming ourselves, I sensed an unusual restlessness in me, something born of my insecurities. What was I really doing in Vihaan's life? What were we doing so far away from everything and everyone?

"Where do you see us going?" I asked Vihaan, unable to keep the question to myself anymore.

Vihaan looked towards the dark mountains beyond us, as if to gather his thoughts, and then turned to look straight into my eyes. "I love you . . ." he said. "I see a future together, with you, but I cannot tell you when that future will be ours to live through . . ."

I nodded. I had dreaded hearing those words again. Vihaan's confession of love had numbed me. I knew he couldn't really drop everything and be with me. He was about to launch himself into politics and he had a small child at home; he wasn't really in any position to make such a life altering move.

"But there's one thing I am certain of..." Vihaan continued, taking my hand in his, "And that is, I love you."

"Just me?"

Vihaan nodded and I left it at that, too tired to discuss things any further. He came close to me and kissed me. I reciprocated instinctively for a moment before pulling back almost immediately.

That night, Vihaan and I slept on the same bed, but I maintained a distance between us, knowing we couldn't take things any further. Not just yet. I had a disturbed sleep laden with anxieties and worries.

The next morning, we had planned to explore the hills in Lonavala, but instead, we had to rush back to Mumbai rather abruptly because Vihaan had been called in for a panel discussion on a leading news channel about the incumbent government's campaign—India Shining. He could have bunked that but I knew it was important for him to be as visible in the media as possible.

As we drove back, Vihaan held my hand. His reassuring touch left very little to be said. We were in love and madly so, yet I knew that the distance between us would remain for now.

***

Later that afternoon, I confided all that was brewing on my mind to Renu.

"Karmic connection," she said, smiling, "That's what such relationships are formed on. You keep crossing paths with your karmic partner."

Renu's words left me perplexed. Was it really so? Were my recurring encounters with Vihaan, even if I subconsciously wanted them to happen, really happening because of some karmic bond that the two of us shared?

That night, after his TV debate, Vihaan came over and the three of us had dinner together at Renu's place. We wanted to be together, Vihaan and I, but since it was my last night in Mumbai, I didn't want to leave Renu alone either. As it is, I had barely spent any time with her.

We sat around a small dining table, a takeaway Chinese meal spread out before us. Vihaan and I sat across each other, holding hands under the table. It was hard to pretend that we were listening to Renu as she narrated a funny anecdote about a colleague of hers, when all we wanted was to get lost in each other. We had never spoken about what was going to happen after I left Mumbai, where we would meet again or if we would. The night ended with me feeling weighed down by all the unanswered questions inside my head.

Next morning, Vihaan dropped me to the airport. There was someone else with us—Tia. Vihaan was going to drop her to pre-school after dropping me at the airport.

"I've mastered multitasking. I don't think I really have a choice," he said, explaining Tia's presence.

"It's good you brought her along. She's such an angel." I took Tia in my lap and hated myself the very next instant, for it seemed to me, for a fraction of a moment, that this was my family—Vihaan and Tia.

Tia chattered away all the way to the airport and I was glad to be spared of the need to have an adult conversation with Vihaan. As we approached the airport and it was time for Vihaan and me to part again, I hugged him tight, tighter than ever. I didn't want to leave him.

"When are we meeting again?" he asked me.

"I don't know . . . do we need to?"

"What do you mean?" he asked me, taken aback by my response.

Thankfully, I was running out of time. "I'm going to miss the flight unless I leave now," I said, ignoring Vihaan's question. I kissed Tia before putting her back in the back seat. Then I quickly got out of the car, grabbed my suitcase, and walked away.

***

When my flight took off for Bangalore an hour later, I suddenly realised that Vihaan's wife was to return from the US later in the night. I kept wondering then about how he would behave with her upon her return. Would he receive her at the airport? Would they kiss? Would they chat and catch up like they'd really missed each other?

I wondered why these details about Vihaan were bothering me. Maybe it was because while Vihaan could manage multitasking professionally and personally, for me exclusivity mattered. I was not a multitasker, a juggler of things, people, and emotions. I didn't feel anything at all for Aziz anymore. I wanted my life with him to be over in all respects. And I wanted a life partner who could fill the vacuum in my life.

In as much as I needed Vihaan and wanted to be with him all the time, I knew I couldn't meet him again. I didn't want him to suffer. He might not be in a great marriage, but he seemed to have made peace with the situation in his life, unlike me who was so reckless and self-destructive. For his sake, I knew I'd have to stay away from him. And that abrupt goodbye, that walking away from him at the airport had been the beginning of it all.

CHAPTER SIX

Srinagar, March 2004

It was the first week of March. Six weeks had gone by since I had parted from Vihaan. I would be lying if I said I didn't miss him, because I did. Every hour. Every day. He had messaged me a couple of times, asking about the book tour and about how things were at home. I had responded in monosyllables each time, not wanting to create a space where we could renew our conversation. In my heart though, I expected him to call me and reach out to me, to persist in his endeavour to break through the walls I was constantly putting up if he was indeed so sure about us. But the complications of the heart are self-defeating! They keep the distances between people intact.

In Srinagar, I stayed with my father and his new family—his second wife, Noor, and their five-year-old son, Imran—in our old bungalow in Nishat. Initially, I was pretty sure I wouldn't be able to stay with Dad for more than a few days, after all it had been years since we had spent so much time with each other in such proximity and too much had happened in the intervening years. I hadn't heard very kind things about my stepmother either, and when I met her, I didn't find her very different from what I had imagined her to be. She was extremely pretty and quite a bit snooty, but she lacked finesse. She tried to be nice to me but I kept my distance. I developed an instant bond with my stepbrother though. When I was a kid, I'd often pester my parents for a younger brother. I would've never thought that Dad would finally fulfil my wish through Imran.

I spent quite a bit of time with Imran, playing with him in the garden and listening to him talk. We would often end up having long conversations and it was through Imran that I realised just how drastically Kashmir had changed over the years. Unlike how things in our childhood had been, when we could walk on the streets and go just about anywhere without any fear, the kids in the valley were now largely confined indoors or sent out only with elders, never alone. Though a large part of Kashmir seemed to be supporting the separatists, almost everyone lived in fear of the extremist elements. It wasn't unheard of for young boys to be kidnapped and smuggled into POK where they were then forced to take up arms against India.

I felt bad for the way children were growing up in an atmosphere of seclusion and fear in a land that had so much to give. How I wished Imran could have a fraction of the carefree childhood that I had had in Srinagar. But for the time being, it seemed that Imran had a wish fulfilled in having me, an unexpected sibling, around to play with as much as he wanted.

My return to Kashmir was also important because it was a chance for me to really know more about my father. Who was he really? The man whom I knew growing up, the one who used to dote on me? Or the man he had come to be—a pro-separatist ideologue? Was his transformation the result of the influence of his new life partner or was it really a genuine change in beliefs and ideology?

Over breakfasts and dinners, I'd have heart-to-heart chats with him, trying to understand his mind.

"You know Zaira, nothing in this world is constant. Everything changes—human nature, bonds, feelings, priorities, thinking, everything. In your youth, you tend to be aspirational and want certain things out of life. But as you grow old and you realise that you haven't got what you aspired for, disillusionment starts setting in. And that's exactly what happened with my feelings towards India . . . when I was growing up, I guess I had expected a lot from the country. But today I feel convinced that Kashmir can never really melt seamlessly into India. Kashmir will forever be like that stepson who is treated shoddily, like an outcast."

"But why do you think like this? Has India ever differentiated against the people of Kashmir? Has India not taken good care of us?" I asked. Dad had been a part of the Hurriyat Conference for some time now and they had been meeting the Indian leadership lately to explore peaceful solutions for the turmoil in the valley. His scepticism, therefore, confused me even further.

"That's our problem. India always tried buying our loyalty with economic incentives and we got bullied into it. We have behaved like opportunists who will swing either way. At least in the last two or three years, there is revived hope because of Atal Bihari Vajpayee. He genuinely seems to mean well for the valley and is talking to all the factions involved. But other than him, we don't trust most Indian leaders. They have all used and abused us."

I realised that every time Dad spoke of India, he almost made it sound like it was a separate country, a country to which

Kashmir did not belong. Even though he was considered a soft separatist, I could see Dad was pretty clear about the direction he saw Kashmir's future taking.

As I lay on my bed later that day, Dad's words about youthful aspirations and disillusionment setting in with age kept echoing in my ears. I could see it happening with me. Ten years ago, I couldn't have imagined I'd fall for Vihaan, a married man, again. Today, it was an inescapable reality that I had to negotiate.

Meanwhile, Aziz had called me just twice ever since I had landed in India. The first call was on the day of the book launch to congratulate me. I was surprised he even remembered the date of the launch. The second call was on 15th February to wish me on my birthday. As for me, I had called him only once in between, a couple of days after I landed in Kashmir. I guess I had been feeling incredibly lonely seeing Dad ensconced with his new family. In all the three phone calls, our conversations had been brief, stilted, and difficult. We had really run out of things to say to each other.

The only good thing that had happened in the past few weeks was my book steadily climbing up the best-sellers list and gaining stronger ground with every passing day. I would get frequent interview requests from the media and I would take these interviews either on mail or on the phone. My publisher too, wanted to capitalise on the book's success and had urged me to start writing my next book. So I started squeezing in a few hours of writing every day in the garden, in between talking to Dad and Imran.

I also started going for long walks alone and visiting places I had fond memories of. On one such walk, I landed up outside my alma mater, Mallinson Girls School, and met a couple of my old teachers. This was where I had attended my kindergarten. And this was where I had fallen in love with Yash. There were so many memories clamouring for attention as I walked through the corridors of the school; some were vivid, but most were faded. Not all of them were fond enough for me to savour them and they only reminded me of my saga of losses. Before they could depress me any further, I hurried out of the building and quickly made my way to the Dal Lake, where, following an impulse, I went on a two-hour-long shikara ride, all alone.

The gentle movement of the shikara, the sound of the oars hitting the water, everything soothed me and I felt the weight of those memories recede. I let my mind drift from thought to thought and by the end of the ride, I had penned down my thoughts in a poem on my phone:

Evening spring breeze
carries mixed fragrances
of the rain-kissed earth, the crackling firewood,
countryside night sky,
filled with soulful music and
dancing lilacs
spicy stew and sweet treats,
unusual essence so familiar
I breathe in this intoxicating smell
and think of you dear.

At night, as the house settled down around me, I'd often wonder about what it was that had kept me in Kashmir for over a month now when I couldn't really escape my melancholia no matter what I did. I wasn't exactly happy being in Kashmir. I wanted to escape from it. But then I also wanted to escape

Aziz and Vihaan. Ironically, I found being with Dad in Kashmir relatively more tolerable than anything else in my life.

***

For the next two days, I found myself virtually confined to the house. A sporadic incident of violence on the outskirts of Srinagar had led to the death of two suspected militants under 'mysterious circumstances' at the hands of the Indian army. This had led to protests and stone-pelting in the Lal Chowk area in which a police officer had lost his life. Such unforeseen incidents, I was told by my father, would erupt every few weeks, keeping the valley on the edge. The local people, however, had gotten used to such happenings and took it all in their stride.

Since the general elections were round the corner, all the political parties with a stake in the valley naturally wanted to portray themselves as being extra sensitive towards the plight of the people. In the immediate aftermath of the incident, therefore, leaders from different parties busied themselves giving statements to the media and in playing the blame game. Even the ruling party was quick to send a three member fact-finding team to the valley. Apart from meeting the families of those who had died in the incident and a group of local residents, the team from Delhi was also supposed to meet the Hurriyat Conference before flying back to Delhi.

As I read the newspaper article about the fact-finding team, I was stunned to find a familiar name in the list of the three political observers coming from Delhi: Vihaan Shastri!

I found it strange and just a little bit upsetting that Vihaan hadn't messaged me about coming to Srinagar. Granted, I hadn't kept our communication channels open, but he was coming to

Srinagar while he knew I was there! And in all probability, he would even meet my father in the meeting with the Hurriyat!

"Zaira!" Dad called me from behind just then, shaking me out of my thoughts.

"We have a meeting in the afternoon with the team from Delhi. One of the names sounds familiar. Vihaan . . . isn't he your friend from college days? Your mother and I even met him once I think."

I nodded.

"I have been watching him on TV debates lately. He looks promising."

"Yeah . . ."

"You're not in touch with him?"

I shook my head.

"Hmm . . ."

Dad's phone began ringing before he could probe any further and he walked away, chatting with one of his innumerable political contacts.

That whole day I was extremely restless. I wanted to message Vihaan and meet him, but I held myself back with great effort. I didn't want to be so weak. I had decided to stay out of his life when I had left Mumbai and I wanted to stay true to my decision, no matter what the situation. But just knowing that he was in the same city as me, just a phone call away, was weakening my resolve. I sat with my phone in my hand all day, waiting for the screen to light up with a message or a call from him, wanting Vihaan to make the move again, but the phone remained silent. I hated Vihaan. I loved him.

Late in the evening when Dad came back, I was sitting in the living room, trying to get some work done on my next manuscript.

"How was your meeting?" I asked him in a dispassionate voice.

"Good, good! It was good," he smiled. "I met Vihaan, very briefly though. He recognised me, after all these years, and came over to greet me. But since there were so many people around, we could barely talk."

"Hmmm . . . have they left for Delhi?"

"I think they were supposed to fly back in the evening. Should have left by now."

I couldn't hold myself back then. I had to talk to Vihaan before he left. Quickly excusing myself, I rushed into my room and called Vihaan but he didn't answer my call.

That night, as we sat having a quiet dinner, our housekeeper informed us that there was a visitor. Wondering who it could be so late in the evening, both Dad and I got up to check. To my disbelief, it was Vihaan.

"I-I-I thought I should come and meet you, and Uncle," Vihaan stammered an explanation right away.

"You knew our address?" Dad asked, just as surprised as me to find Vihaan in our drawing room.

"Everybody in Srinagar knows where you live," he replied.

"But I thought you had an evening flight back?" Dad queried.

"Yes, b-b-but I felt like missing it. I mean, I missed it. I am going back tomorrow morning now," he fumbled, clearly distracted.

"Anyway, come in, come in . . ." Dad ushered Vihaan in, "we were just having our dinner . . . join us!"

"This must be an auspicious day," Dad joked as we settled back at the dinner table. "It's not every day that you find a leader from the ruling nationalist party dining at the house of a separatist!"

Chapter Six: Srinagar, March 2004

"Well, Uncle, I am not yet a leader. I am just about finding my way," Vihaan smiled.

"You know Vihaan, the first time I met you thirteen years ago, right then and there I knew you'd achieve something big in life . . ." Dad was being very nice to Vihaan.

"But Uncle, how did you end up with the separatists? I mean, you didn't like them at all in the past. In fact you abhorred them!"

"Yes, but did you know then that you'd be in politics one day? No, right? That's life. You don't know what the next chapter is going to be," Dad philosophised before adding, "But I had my valid reasons. I had blindly trusted the Indian leadership for far too long and when things didn't change the way they should have, I began to feel betrayed."

"India has cheated us," Noor intruded.

"No it hasn't," I retorted, shutting her up before Vihaan was forced to respond to her allegation.

Realising the awkwardness of the situation, Dad intervened quickly. "Where are you staying?" he asked Vihaan, changing the subject.

"Well, since I hadn't really planned on staying back,"—Vihaan looked pointedly at me when he said that—"I don't have a hotel room just yet. But I have asked a local party member to get me a hotel room. He should be calling me any moment now to confirm that."

"No, no, no, Vihaan. You are our guest tonight and you will stay with us," Dad insisted, forever the perfect, most hospitable host. "Call your party chap and tell him you are staying with a friend or something. I will make sure nobody knows you stayed in our house. You anyway have to leave for the airport in the morning . . . Besides, you and Zaira will get some time to talk and catch up after so many years!"

Dad wouldn't listen to anything Vihaan said about not being able to stay the night and he completely ignored the disapproving look on his wife's face. So that was that.

***

It was around midnight that Vihaan and I finally found ourselves alone and went out for a stroll in the garden. We hadn't exchanged a single word since the time Vihaan had arrived at our doorstep, but as we walked around the garden, I could sense that Vihaan was feeling somewhat low.

"Hold me, Zaira," he said suddenly, breaking the silence.

Without a word, I turned and embraced him. When you're really intimately bound to someone, even a simple embrace carries a unique chemistry and the physical synchronisation is almost ethereal. And that's how I felt on embracing Vihaan.

To my surprise though, Vihaan sounded emotionally choked when he stepped back after a moment and started to talk.

"I have to tell you something . . . Ritu and I have decided to separate. We had a huge row after she returned from the US and we've hardly been on talking terms since then, communicating only when essential or on issues concerning Tia. But last week, the situation flared up again and then two days ago, she just packed her bags and shifted to her sister's place, taking Tia with her."

"Why didn't you tell me about all this before, Vihaan?!"

"When? When could I tell you about any of this, Zaira? You have hardly spoken to me since you left Mumbai!" Vihaan lashed out at me. "Whenever I messaged you, your answers were all monosyllabic! I could have called, but I didn't get the impression you wanted me to."

Chapter Six: Srinagar, March 2004

"I-I-I am sorry, Vihaan," I whispered. "I had no clue all this was happening in your life . . . I was only avoiding any conversation with you because I needed to keep my own expectations in check . . . I cannot be a passing distraction in anyone's life . . ."

I didn't want to hide my feelings for Vihaan anymore. I knew he was just as emotionally attached to me as he had been thirteen years ago. What I didn't know was what was it exactly that was stopping him from starting his life again with me? Did he still love his wife? Was he scared that the news of his separation and of a parallel romance with me would upset his political aspirations? Did he love Tia so much that he was willing to rather stay put in his marriage till she had grown up? Or was it something about me, my temperamental fickleness perhaps that scared him from making a commitment?

"My decision to move away from Ritu is final, but we might hold off filing for divorce for a few months though, until the elections are over. I cannot afford the scandal of a divorce right before the elections. That'll be a PR disaster," Vihaan explained as we continued walking around the garden, clasping each other's hands.

"But why do I get a feeling that you love her too?" I asked Vihaan bluntly, not entirely convinced by his reasoning.

Vihaan paused before answering my question. "I don't love Ritu, no, but I feel responsible for her, like I feel responsible for everybody else who is a part of my life, like I feel responsible for you . . ."

But I wasn't everybody. I couldn't be everybody. I didn't want to be everybody! My insides were now beginning to scream and rebel for not being given the primacy that I needed in the relationship I had with Vihaan, fraught as it was with complications and strains.

"Let's go to sleep," I said abruptly, wanting to escape the whole conversation. And without waiting for a reply from Vihaan, I turned around and walked towards my room, leaving him alone in the garden. He called out to me but I ignored him.

Of course I couldn't sleep as the hours ticked by. Everything Vihaan had said and everything that I had left unsaid about this perplexing, chaotic relationship hounded me. How I wished we could peep into our future. How I wished we could just switch off emotionally at times. But the human mind with its tumultuous swirl of emotions wasn't a machine that could be switched on and off at will.

Hours later, towards the break of dawn, my restlessness and the fact that Vihaan would once again be gone in a few hours, had me pick up my cell phone.

"Sleeping?" I messaged him.

"No" came the prompt answer.

"Come out to the garden." I messaged back.

Half an hour later, Vihaan and I were on a shikara on the Dal Lake in a desperate bid on my part to steal what limited moments I was destined to have with him.

"Let's celebrate this moment," I told Vihaan, looking at the beautiful view all around us as the boatman started rowing us towards the Chinar trees in the middle of the lake. "Let's not talk about our future . . . let's just live in this moment, on this shikara, as if there is no tomorrow, no real life waiting to claim us back . . ."

"Yes, and if it's destined then soon all the moments in our lives will be like these." Vihaan's words sounded so reassuring that I allowed myself to believe them.

For the next forty minutes, we recalled some of the most precious moments from our past. Vihaan asked me to recite the poem which I had recited at the Hindu College fest where he'd first seen me.

"I still remember every bit of that day. Your nervousness on the stage, the off-white dress that you wore, your eloquence, your words . . . Come on, Zaira, let me hear that poem again!"

I was about to recite the poem for him but I checked myself at the last moment.

"No, I won't recite that poem."

"But why?" Vihaan asked, perplexed.

"Because that was written for someone else.

Then, I recited a poem which I had written barely a week ago when I'd been missing Vihaan acutely:

> *Sometimes, life is not what you want it to be*
> *Sometimes, the path seems too long*
> *The only thought that keeps me going is*
> *you are mine*
>
> *Sometimes, you find yourself standing all alone*
> *Sometimes, there is no one to reach out to*
> *The only thought that keeps me going is*
> *you are mine*
>
> *Sometimes, the colours seem to be fading away*
> *Sometimes, the rainbow is just hiding away*
> *The only thought that keeps me going is*
> *you are mine*
>
> *Sometimes, sunshine is covered with dark clouds*
> *Sometimes, you keep waiting for the silver line*
> *The only thought that keeps me going is*
> *you are mine*

Come and hold my hand again
Come and touch my soul again
I am lonely without you
Let the sun shine and make me come alive.

It was a pleasant providence that the last sentence of my poem coincided with the sun breaking through the clouds and shining bright upon us.

"I love you," Vihaan said when I was done.

"I-I . . . lo . . ." I looked away, unable to bring myself to say those words, not when everything was so uncertain between us.

I don't know if Vihaan understood the reasons behind my hesitation, but he didn't say anything for the longest while until, unable to bear the silence any longer, I absurdly asked him to give one of his political speeches in front of me. Vihaan obliged and delivered a speech which was high on promises. It left me damn impressed, even though I wondered for a moment if there was any premium attached for a politician in fulfilling promises. I wanted to believe he was not a politician at heart.

Towards the end of our shikara ride, both Vihaan and I literally went berserk singing Hindi film songs. Vihaan flattered me by matching Shammi Kapoor's energy and singing *Yeh chand sa raushan chehra, zulfon ka raang sunehra* from the film *Kashmir ki Kali*. I couldn't help but burst out laughing at his antics. I wished I could respond as demurely as Sharmila Tagore to his compliments! But the only song I could come up with in response was *Pardesiyon se na akhiyaan milana . . . Pardesiyon ko hai ek din jaana . . .*

With the shikara ride about to end, I asked the boatman to click a few pictures of Vihaan and me from my cell phone. He readily obliged with a smile.

Chapter Six: Srinagar, March 2004

"I have ferried hundreds of couples but there's something very special between the two of you," he remarked.

"What?" asked Vihaan.

"The craving that you have for each other . . . it's like you have been together always and will always be together . . . nothing will keep you away from each other for too long."

The boatman's words sounded almost prophetic and jolted both Vihaan and me back into the real world, a world where both of us still had a lot of distance to tread before we could legitimately belong to each other.

An hour later, we stood waiting at the gate for Vihaan's taxi.

"There is this one wish of mine that remains unfulfilled," I remembered suddenly.

Vihaan looked at me, trying to decipher what was on my mind.

"The bike ride from Srinagar to Pahalgam," I told him, laughing.

Vihaan broke into laughter as well. "I'm feeling confident now that it will happen soon," he said, caressing my hair.

The taxi drew up just then and I instinctively tightened my hold on Vihaan's hand. I didn't want to let go of him. Not just yet. "You take care," I said, straightening his dishevelled hair and trying hard not to give in to the tears that were beginning to spill.

"You too," Vihaan said softly, hugging me and kissing my forehead.

And then he was gone.

***

In the weeks after Vihaan went back to Mumbai, we stayed in touch on a regular basis. He'd call me usually at night to have a long chat, but even through the day we'd exchange messages and talk when we felt like it. Those few hours that Vihaan and I had spent together when he'd come to see me had changed something between us. We still weren't sure about a future together but I knew there was no point in forcibly removing myself from Vihaan's life anymore, not when our paths were destined to meet again and again.

I would normally wait for him to message me because I knew he was keeping extremely busy with the elections just round the corner. And somewhere in some twisted mind game that I played with myself, I also wanted to see if he would make time for me in his hectic schedule.

"Ritu has come back to the house. Tia wasn't keeping well and I wanted to be around her. Tia sleeps with me in my room. Ritu and I live in separate rooms though," Vihaan updated me one night, explaining the details of his domestic arrangement without me having asked for them. But I would be lying if I said I wasn't insecure and that Vihaan's words didn't reassure me a little. I had lost enough in life and I couldn't afford to lose more. Unlike Vihaan, I wasn't really entangled in a web of complications with Aziz. For me, it was a matter of initiating the legal process of ending things between us. But things were different for Vihaan and until he was out of his messy marriage, I couldn't be sure about where we were really headed. I needed all the words and gestures of reassurance that I could find in the meanwhile. To be fair to Vihaan, despite him grappling with new challenges and being under so much pressure, he somehow understood my insecurities, almost intuitively so. He made efforts to be in constant touch and to involve me in his life as much as possible. That meant a lot to me.

I knew Vihaan was really stressed. All the major political parties had started announcing their candidates for the upcoming elections. Vihaan had been eyeing Varanasi, his hometown, and even though there were two other senior contenders for the seat, he was hoping to scrape through and get a nomination.

"Just maintain your calm. All will be well," I assured him. I wasn't in any position to do anything beyond that. I had started praying for him every day. I'd chant *Nam Myoho Renge Kyo*, a Buddhist chant I had learned from a Buddhist friend in Kenya, wishing that Vihaan's aspirations get fulfilled and that our hopes of a future together fructify.

Then suddenly one day in the middle of the afternoon, my phone rang. To my surprise, it was Vihaan. I was too taken aback by the sudden call. Vihaan wouldn't call during the day, not unless he had some news, some important new. But I didn't take the call immediately. Instead, I quickly chanted *Nam Myoho Renge Kyo* for a couple of minutes, gathering myself. Then I called him back.

"Zaira! I have a couple of things to share with you," Vihaan said the moment he answered my call, his voice brimming with energy. "The good news is that I've been given the party ticket from the Ghazipur constituency. Varanasi couldn't happen, but Ghazipur is a neighbouring constituency."

"Wow!" I released the breath I hadn't realised I was holding. "I'm so happy for you, Vihaan."

"Thanks Zaira . . . thanks for being there."

"Oh Viha—"

"Wait, wait," Vihaan cut me short. "There's another bit of news," he sounded stressed now. "Ritu and I had a huge fight last night. I can't stand her anymore, not even for a single day. She's gone off to her sister's house again and I don't want her to come back. I've decided to divorce her."

"Oh!" I didn't know what else to say. I didn't know how I was expected to react to what Vihaan had just said. I was afraid to believe that it was finally happening.

"I'll be travelling to Ghazipur tomorrow to file my nomination papers," Vihaan continued, "and after that, I will make Delhi and Ghazipur my base for the next few weeks. Tia will be in Mumbai with Ritu . . . I will be living alone in Delhi . . ."

"I will see you in Delhi day after tomorrow evening," I told Vihaan, understanding what he was really trying to tell me and knowing how much he had begun to depend on me.

Vihaan was ecstatic when he heard this. "I love you," he said.

"I know . . ." I whispered.

"Do you?" he asked me.

"Why should I tell you?" I teased him, unable to contain my laughter.

***

That night, I had a long chat with Dad as the two of us sat around the small bonfire in the garden. I finally confided in him and told him everything about the relationship between Vihaan and me. I knew he would never judge me, but what never ceased to surprise me was how easily he could shift from being a father to a friend every time I needed him as one.

"Hmm . . ." he smiled when I finished narrating everything. "What a fascinating story it is, isn't it?"

"Yeah . . . I guess so . . ."

Chapter Six: Srinagar, March 2004

"But honestly speaking, Zaira, I am not really surprised. I always knew you had my romantic genes. But what are you going to do now?"

"I think I should be with Vihaan at this juncture. He needs me."

"Hmmm . . . so back to Delhi tomorrow then, right?"

I nodded, hugging him. I sent up a silent prayer of thanks for being lucky enough to have a father who didn't pressurise me to go back to my husband, but who, instead, let me follow my heart.

Dad then went one step ahead and called his cousin brother, Asad, in Delhi. Asad Uncle used to be my local guardian in my college days. He and Dad shared a thick bond. Dad, being his protective self, simply briefed him about my situation. Asad Uncle managed to conceal his shock and much to my surprise, said that he would be happy to host me in his Safdurjung Enclave house.

When Dad dropped me to the airport the next day, I held on to him for a long moment, drawing strength from him. His politics aside, if there was anyone in the world who understood me completely and so intuitively, it was him. My mother and I had drifted apart a long time ago and save for that one phone call every year on Christmas, we hardly ever spoke. I could never imagine telling her about Vihaan as I had told Dad. Even though I didn't particularly like Noor, I now understood some bits of what Dad must have gone through to gather the courage to start anew after his divorce from Mom. I needed to find that same courage within myself and the time that I had spent with him had given me the push that I had needed.

***

It was late evening by the time I reached Asad Uncle's house in Safdurjung Enclave. I knew Vihaan was in Ghazipur, filing his nomination papers. I had wanted to be with him when he filed his nomination, but I knew that was an imprudent thought; after all, our relationship did not have either the name or the legitimacy which we needed for me to be able to do something like that.

I had a quick dinner with Asad Uncle and retired early to my room, feeling a little tired. I lay on the bed and switched on the TV, thinking it would distract me from dwelling too much on everything that was going. As I surfed through the news channels, I wasn't in the least prepared for the shock I was going to get.

It was a visual of Vihaan filing his nomination papers at the district commissioner's office in Ghazipur, and standing next to him was Ritu, draped in a sari, looking every bit the dutiful, supportive housewife.

I couldn't believe my eyes. What was Ritu doing there with Vihaan? How could they look like they were a perfectly happy couple, still very much in love with each other?

"How much has your wife contributed in your life?" the news channel reporter asked Vihaan in the interview that followed.

"I've led an uncertain life, chasing my ambitions and trying to balance my personal life. This journey would not have been possible without Ritu's support and understanding."

I switched off the TV, completely shocked. I could feel a heaviness in my head and a thundering sound beginning to fill my ears. My heart started palpitating. It was happening again. The world was crumbling around me and I was powerless to stop it. All I could do was lock myself in the room and stumble to the bed.

Chapter Six: Srinagar, March 2004

At some point in time my phone began to ring. I could see Vihaan's name flashing on the screen. But I did not pick up the phone; instead I put it on silent mode and let it ring. Perhaps Vihaan had realised that I might have seen the interview. Perhaps he wanted to give me some kind of an explanation, a justification, for Ritu's presence in Ghazipur and for his words in the interview. But I wasn't prepared to talk to him or anyone else for that matter. Never had I felt as betrayed and let down as I did then.

By midnight there were fifty-seven missed calls from Vihaan and also a few desperate messages:

> "Listen Zaira, I need to talk to you. Whatever you saw on TV, it was all a facade. The truth is, I love you . . ."
>
> "For God's sake, Zaira, talk to me. Pick up my call! I will tell you everything."
>
> "Zaira, I love you, just you . . . hear me out. Please don't do this, not again. Don't shut me out."

At that point in time, I called up my cell phone operator and had Vihaan's number blocked.

Two days later, I flew back to Mexico to end things formally with Aziz. That chapter had to be closed legally. I knew my life was headed towards a gaping hole but I somehow felt prepared to embrace it.

A month later, even as I relocated to London and shuffled between London and Mexico City for my divorce proceedings, I read on the Internet that Vihaan had won the elections from Ghazipur by a decent margin of six-thousand votes. He was now a Member of Parliament. He had sent a couple of emails to me, wanting to talk about what had happened on the day of his filing the nomination papers and to explain things to me, but I didn't respond to any of his overtures. I was tempted to talk to him, yes, but I knew I had to be ruthless with myself in order to contain my own expectations and move on. I had realised by now that he was the one I truly loved, but if he was not destined to be mine then I would much rather cut myself off from him completely than let there be lingering traces of a connection.

PART THREE

VIHAAN: PAST IMPERFECT FUTURE TENSE

CHAPTER SEVEN

New Delhi, September 2016

At 6:30 p.m., at Gulmohar hall in India Habitat Centre, Zaira was ready to launch her new book, *A Chequered Life*. Zaira was now a well-known, London-based writer, having created a mark for herself with her unconventional romantic stories of unrequited love. I had read two of her books so far and had found both of them to have been written with such passion that even a cynic would have greedily lapped up her words and finished the books in one sitting.

When I entered the hall, the book had already been released and Zaira was reading out an excerpt from the book, looking up from time to time to gauge the audience's reaction to her words, not that she needed to worry about that, hooked as they all were to the story. She saw me walk in and faltered for a moment before resuming her reading. There was no reason for her to recognise me since I was wearing a disguise—a salt and pepper beard and a hat. But something made Zaira look right at me again as I made my way to an empty third-row seat. I looked the other way immediately, not wanting to give anything away.

Ever since Zaira had snapped off all ties with me yet again in 2004, we had never met again. What little I knew about her was from news snippets from here and there about her as an upcoming Indian writer. But there were never any details about her personal life in any of the news items. I guess whatever she knew about me now, if she did at all, would also be from newspapers and television. My life had changed drastically after the 2004 elections. Even though my party had lost the elections, I made my mark as an active MP from Ghazipur. I wasn't anonymous anymore; my life had been thrown open to public gaze. And a year after my becoming an MP, when I divorced Ritu, the news found wide circulation in the press. I knew that despite her best efforts to shut me out of her life, Zaira couldn't have been totally unaware of my divorce. In all the time that had passed since then, I often wondered why she never got in touch with me after my divorce. Did she never empathise with me? Did she never understand that I had been trapped in a genuinely complicated situation?

I guess our relationship had already become so burdened by ill-timing and failures by then that she just did not have it in her to make her way out of another misunderstanding. Perhaps she just gave up on us. Besides, after my initial attempts to get in touch with her I never really tried much to get through to her. I began to tell myself that if she were meant to stay in my life and be a part of it, she'd make her way back in.

But somewhere deep inside, I felt more than a little let down by Zaira's unilateral exit from my life and her refusal to talk to me. She could have shown a little more faith in me. After all, she knew I had, and have, always loved her. That should have been reason enough. A part of me had even concluded that Zaira's cynicism had made her an inveterate escapist and that she could probably never be steady in a relationship.

Chapter Seven: New Delhi, September 2016

But that's how complicated love can be, as they say. Destiny had conspired to keep us away for the last twelve years, until Zaira's publisher, for whatever reason, ended up sending an invitation for her book launch to me. At this stage in my life I could never really go anywhere, leave alone to a function, without my Z+ security cover, but here I had reasons to behave differently. My restlessness had returned when I'd seen that invite, as had my quest for answers. I didn't want to die with the most important questions about my life remaining unanswered.

Once the book reading was done, Zaira came down from the stage and began signing copies of her book. Since a pretty large number of people had turned up for the event, there was quite a long line of people waiting to get their copies signed. I stood patiently at the end of the queue after purchasing a copy of Zaira's book from the makeshift stall at the back of the hall. I was a little nervous because the thing about meeting someone you have really truly loved is that no matter how much you convince yourself that you have moved on, in reality you haven't actually moved an inch. There are latent anxieties and insecurities which suddenly erupt out of nowhere. You are not sure whether you can talk to her with the same intimacy as before. You don't know whether to pretend that the past never happened or to acknowledge it after all the years in between.

After about twenty minutes of waiting and wondering what to say, when I was finally in front of Zaira, I didn't have to utter a word. Zaira intuitively identified me the minute I held out the copy of her book for her to sign.

"Vihaan?"

"Con-con-congratulations, Zaira!" I said, my words faltering in anticipation and nervousness. "It's been a long time . . ." God, she was still just as beautiful as the first day I had seen her.

Zaira didn't say anything. She looked awkward and nervous. Perhaps with everybody looking at her she didn't want me, an entanglement from her past, to disrupt her present and shift the focus away from her book. As she hurriedly signed my copy, still looking undecided about what to say to me, she was asked aside by her publisher as a TV channel wanted to record an interview with her.

"I am sorry. You'll have to excuse me," she said rather curtly and walked away, looking rather relieved at having escaped me.

I stood where I was, staring at her retreating back, hurt by the impersonal manner in which she had treated me. She hadn't asked me to wait for her or said that she would talk to me later. She had just walked away. As if I were just another man in the crowd. Of course I knew that a book launch event was no place to have a personal conversation, but she didn't have to act so cold, so indifferent.

As I began moving out of the hall, confused and a little angry, I bumped into Renu, Zaira's friend. But Renu didn't recognise me, not until I took her aside and revealed my identity.

Unlike Zaira, Renu was warm and friendly. We had a quick chat, catching up. She even congratulated me on my political successes. Though still based out of Mumbai, she was there for Zaira, like always, clubbing an official trip to coincide with Zaira's book launch. I was tempted to ask her about Zaira, but I held myself back. Before leaving, as we exchanged phone numbers and promises to keep in touch, Renu casually mentioned that Zaira would be in Delhi for the next few months, she had joined the guest faculty of a new private university on the outskirts of Gurgaon.

Chapter Seven: New Delhi, September 2016

So, fate had brought us near each other again. But before I could react, I got an urgent call on my hotline number. The call was from the prime minister.

***

It was 12:30 a.m. and at 7, Lok Kalyan Marg, the official residence of the prime minister, a small group was locked in an intense meeting. It included the PM, Vaibhav Patel, the home minister, Siddharth Gupta, all the three chiefs of the armed forces, the national security advisor (NSA), the DGMO, and me.

"The public is restive this time. We have to give it back to Pakistan and give it back hard," insisted the home minister.

The PM nodded before turning towards me.

"Are we ready with options?" he asked.

"Yes sir," I replied and opened the file the army chief handed to me. "We have two options, sir. The first is an army-led surgical strike. The second is also an army-led surgical strike, but coupled with an attack by the navy in the Arabian Sea." The proposal of a naval attack surprised the home minister and the PM. "Sir," I continued, "the second option is the best under the circumstances. It will be a first and it will distract the Pakistani establishment greatly and provide a perfect opportunity for our army to teach them a lesson over a couple of hours."

"But have we factored in all the possible repercussions?" asked the PM.

The NSA took over then and explained the possible fallouts. "The key would be in limiting the duration of this attack," he said, answering the last of the PM's questions. "We will need to be done with the whole operation in two to three hours."

"And of course, our external affairs minister and the diplomats in all the relevant countries will be briefed on the immediate steps," I elaborated.

"I don't think using the navy simultaneously is a good idea," the home minister chipped in before the PM could say anything. "It is fraught with too many risks."

"But aren't we supposed to retaliate unpredictably? I mean we need to do something which jolts the enemy this time!"

This led to a bit of an argument between Siddharth and I, with both of us putting up a strong case and debating heatedly.

"Let's go with the army-led surgical strike for now," the PM asserted finally. "But hit them really hard and do it on a dark night."

***

Four nights later, on a moonless night, the army carried out a meticulously planned attack on several spots along the Line of Control. Hours later, through a press conference addressed by the DGMO, news about this surgical strike was released to the public. The press release had been very carefully worded and I had approved of it:

Based on specific and credible inputs that some terrorist teams had positioned themselves at launch pads along the Line of Control with the intention of infiltrating and conducting terrorist strikes inside Jammu and Kashmir and in various metros in other states, the Indian army conducted surgical strikes at several of these launch pads as a pre-emptive counter measure. The entire operation was focussed on ensuring that these terrorists do not

Chapter Seven: New Delhi, September 2016

succeed in their design to cause destruction and endanger the lives of our citizens.

During this operation, significant casualties have been reported among the terrorists and those providing support to them.

The operation has since ceased. We do not have any further plans to continue with such strikes. However, the armed forces of the nation are fully prepared for any contingency that may arise as a response to these surgical strikes.

Even though the surgical strikes signalled a part closure to the Gurez attacks from the Indian side, as the defence minister, the pressure on me had only increased. There was no way one could anticipate how Pakistan would respond. Hence, the army, the air force, and the navy were all put on high alert. I spent the next three days at my South Block office, closely monitoring the situation and looking more and more like a zombie. On the fourth day, with there being still no sign of an immediate response from Pakistan, I finally decided to return home.

My eyes were red from lack of sleep and I was grappling with a bad headache. All I wanted was a few hours of sleep. But my mind . . . my mind was in too much of a chaos to grant me that. Images of Zaira from the book launch and memories of our time together were back to haunt me.

I really wanted to talk to Zaira and the more I thought about it, the stronger was the craving to hear her voice. Finally, quite late in the evening, I called up Renu. She sounded surprised when she picked up my call.

"Vihaan! What are you doing calling me? I would've thought

you'd be knee-deep in closed-door meetings and briefings and what not! Is everything okay?" she asked.

Without beating around the bush, I asked Renu right away for Zaira's number. For a moment Renu dithered, unsure about whether she should give me Zaira's number without asking her, but then she relented—perhaps she felt bad for me, or perhaps she knew enough about Zaira and me—and gave me Zaira's number.

An hour later I was still struggling with what to type in the message to Zaira. Exasperated with my own self, I finally wrote "Hi Zaira, how are you? Vihaan" and sent it.

With no response for the next forty minutes, my anxieties grew. I realised I didn't have the patience to wait for a text response. I wanted to call Zaira and talk to her. I felt like telling her how much I missed her. Instead, I settled for a very sober message.

"It's okay to not answer. Take care. Goodnight."

Five minutes later, my phone beeped.

"I'm good, Vihaan. Hope you're fine. Take Care. Goodnight."

Zaira's message did not leave any scope for further conversation. But it was an opening at least.

Two days later I messaged her again in the middle of a five-minute break at work.

"Zaira, can we talk please?"

The reply came many hours later at night.

"We can."

I realised Zaira was perhaps deliberately being curt. But I did not really care about that. All I wanted was to talk to her again. So I called her.

Chapter Seven: New Delhi, September 2016

"I want to meet you . . ." I said the moment she picked up the phone.

An uncertain silence followed.

"Ah . . . well you know, I'm not up for it."

"Listen, Zaira, I need to talk to you . . ." I persisted.

"Then talk."

"Right . . . actually, I think I'll call you again when you're in a better mood. Bye Zaira."

My secretary, Mahesh Rana, had known me for years and he knew about everything that went on in my life. He had walked into my room just as I was hanging up the phone and on realising it was Zaira I was talking to, he looked at me sceptically.

"Sir, you are treading on dangerous waters here," he warned me. "Even though Bilal Mohammed Bhat has been quiet for the last couple of years, he is still being closely monitored by the IB . . ."

I nodded, not unaware of the situation. Zaira's father, although in hiding now, was a Hurriyat leader with suspected ties to terrorist outfits across the border. He was certainly not the kind of man the defence minister of a country could afford to be connected to in any manner. And here I was, wanting to renew my relationship with his daughter.

Mahesh's caveat stayed on my mind. Was I so emotionally helpless when it came to Zaira that I would take a risk like that? I had faith in Zaira's integrity, yes. I knew she could never be a part of her father's anti-India agenda even remotely. But did I really need to trap myself in this dilemma between duty and love?

A month went by. I had hoped that Zaira would message or call me back. But she didn't. And with every passing day, my anxieties only increased. I realised at the end of that one month of daily disappointment over Zaira's silence, that this persistent anxiety, if left uncontrolled, would soon take its toll on my work and on my metal state. And one night, when sleep eluded me completely, I sat up and wrote a long email to Zaira. I just had to tell her the truth. Irrespective of whether she wanted to know it or not, it was imperative for me to get it out of my system now.

Zaira, I know you still feel betrayed by what happened in Ghazipur. But you need to know the truth. It's not that I didn't want to communicate all of this to you earlier, but the way you shunted me out of your life, I just didn't know whether you were interested to know anything at all. And so, after the first few months of trying to reach you, I gave up. But today I want to tell you everything. Whether you read this email or not, whether you believe me or not is a choice you will make. But I need to put the truth out there, between us.

Two days before I actually filed my nomination papers in 2004, the day I called you, if you remember, I went to Ritu to talk to her about our divorce. Ritu surprised me by being apologetic about everything that had happened and by asking me to give our marriage another try. I told her, in no uncertain terms, that that wouldn't happen, but she was insistent that we hold off at least until the elections were over. Restless and confused, I spoke to my political mentor, who is also a party senior. He strongly advised me not to let the media even get a whiff of my failed marriage. It would prove detrimental to my image in a small, orthodox town like Ghazipur. At least wait until the elections are over and then go about it quietly, he said. So I played along. I had too much at stake to go against his advice. On the day I was to travel to

Chapter Seven: New Delhi, September 2016

Ghazipur, Ritu surprised me yet again by saying that she wanted to accompany me for the campaigning. I couldn't stop her in all the chaos that was going on, but I hoped, I really hoped that I would get a chance to explain the situation to you ASAP. But as luck would have it, throughout the day I remained surrounded by people and before I could speak to you, the TV footage had already written a different story. I knew you would see it. And I knew how you would interpret it. I won the election, but I lost you.

Two months later, Ritu's firm went in for a merger with an American venture capital fund. I was then shocked to discover that Ritu had been playing me along with her reconciliatory overtures. The American venture capital fund had gone ahead with the merger because it had been influenced by the perception that I was a protégé of the then finance minister, Ashok Pandey. They had been led to believe that with our party presumed to retain power, I could be of strategic help to them gaining stronger hold in the Indian market. Ritu, being the wily operator that she was, had wanted to delay the divorce for as long as possible because I was the trump card her firm held, and her firm badly needed this merger.

Ritu and I had always had temperamental differences but this morbid act of manipulation and deception was the last straw for me. It made it clear to me that our differences were irreconcilable. I filed for a divorce almost immediately, and a year after I became an MP, I was a free man. I tried reaching out to you but you had blocked me from your email ids and had changed your number as well. You made sure that there was literally no way I could reach you. When a person does something like that, you can interpret it in many ways. I was, and have, always been insecure about you.

I thought that perhaps you had found happiness elsewhere. So I retreated and buried myself in my work. But the fact is Zaira, I could never stop thinking about you. I could never stop believing that we'd meet again. And we did. After twelve long years.

Zaira, I need you to know that I have never let you down consciously. I would never do that. Whatever happened back in 2004, whatever misunderstandings have kept us apart, let's just forget about them now . . . let's be there for each other, please . . .

Always yours,

Vihaan

Next morning I called up Renu and took Zaira's email id from her. Before I ended the brief conversation, I asked her something which had been bothering me for some time now.

"Renu, is there a man in Zaira's life?"

"Sorry?"

"Ah . . . w-well . . . is she seeing someone?"

"No," Renu replied, laughing.

***

The response, when it came a couple of days later, was unexpectedly phlegmatic. But I knew then that it was the opening I had been looking for. After that, it took me four more months of sustained pestering to have Zaira acquiesce to meet me. Interestingly, it was on her birthday that we met again.

We met for dinner at Hotel Ashoka. Fully aware of the need for secrecy, I had Zaira come to an executive suite on the seventh floor. I had thought of calling Zaira home but I knew she would be more comfortable in a neutral venue.

As Zaira entered the suite, it seemed as if everything that had kept us apart, it all suddenly crumbled and fell away. I walked up to her and hugged her.

"Happy birthday, Zaira!" I whispered, pulling back after a minute and kissing her on her forehead.

"Thank you, but you really didn't have to do all this," Zaira said, gesturing to the chocolate truffle cake on the table in front of us. I had especially asked for it, knowing it was her favourite flavour.

"Well, fate has been rather stingy in giving us time together. It is your birthday today, the second one I get to spend with you . . . it's the least I could do . . ."

"How have you been?" Zaira asked me as we sat down and I poured us some wine.

"Good," I replied and added after a pause, "But somewhat incomplete . . ."

I turned and held Zaira's hand, caressing it gently.

"Why didn't you get in touch with me? Why did you block me off like that? I'm sure you knew I was divorced . . . all these years that we lost, Zaira . . ."

"I was confident that *you* would reach out to me . . ."

"I tried, Zaira. I tried for months before I gave up. Besides, you were still married to Aziz, weren't you?"

Zaira shook her head. "I divorced Aziz immediately after returning to Mexico. If you had really wanted to reach out, Vihaan, you would have managed to find a way, like you did now . . ."

I was left speechless. Was I indeed guilty of not trying hard enough to reach out to Zaira? Had my political ambition made me sceptical of chasing an elusive romance?

"How old is Tia? She must have grown up into a lovely young girl now. . ." Zaira asked, changing the subject.

We chatted then like old friends do, catching up on life, talking about this and that. Zaira mentioned in passing that after the present teaching semester ended in the coming month, she planned to travel to Kashmir and stay there for a few months to write her next book.

We parted an hour later, for that was all the time that I had. Our partings had always been melancholic for me. I had hated returning to my hostel after every meeting with Zaira back when we were in college, and I hated going home now. I never knew what the next day would bring for Zaira and me.

When I went to bed some hours later, my cell phone beeped. It was a message from Zaira.

"It was lovely meeting you . . . I appreciate your efforts in making me feel special today. And sorry if I've been acting tough . . ."

I suddenly felt relaxed. That's the magic of the positive vibe of someone you hold dear. I called up Tia and chatted with her for a good half hour after that, asking her about her studies and her friends.

"Dad, you sound so relaxed after months. Usually you are so spaced out and tired!" remarked Tia.

That night, after months, I went to bed with a calm mind and with a smile on my face.

When I woke up though, I was in for an incredibly rude shock. The TOI had carried a damning, front page article about my romance with Zaira, the daughter of separatist leader, Bilal Mohammed Bhat. Somehow, they had also managed to get hold of two pictures to support the story. One was from the book launch and the other was from 2004, when I had visited Zaira's family in Srinagar. The headline of this explosive cover story was: *What's Cooking Between the Defence Minister and the Separatist Leader's Daughter?*

I couldn't believe my eyes. I knew the biggest crisis of my life was staring right at me and that I'd have to pay a huge price for this. And yet, beyond the initial jittery moments, I didn't feel scared about the repercussion. Rather, I felt brave, like I had never felt before. This, I felt sure, was the accumulated strength of my love for my country and for the only woman I had loved in life.

CHAPTER EIGHT

New Delhi, February 2017

I stood in front of the prime minister, uncertain and nervous about what he would say to me.

"Sit down," he said without looking up from the file he was studying.

I sat down. My mind was still in a tizzy over the newspaper article. Even before I had had time to assess the damage done by the article, I had been summoned to the PM's office for an urgent meeting. With my own mind caught up in a flurry of thoughts about Zaira and my karmic connection with her, for the first time I wasn't confident about whether I'd be able to answer the questions the PM was sure to ask me.

The PM finally looked up after fifteen minutes. He stared at me, making me want to squirm in my chair, like a small boy in the principal's office.

"So tell me what happened," he said, coming straight to the point.

"Sir, I am sorry about this newspaper report. I-I know it has caused much embarrassment to the government—"

"Are you sorry about the report or about what you've done?" the PM cut me short.

I took a moment before I responded to his pointed question. "Just about the report, sir. My feelings for Zaira will never impinge on my duties as the defence minister of India. I never have and never will compromise on our national interests."

"I'm sure you know that politics is a game of perception?"

"I do, sir."

"Well then, take your time and think about your priorities. I will wait for you to come back to me on how you propose to salvage the situation. Meanwhile, don't interact with the press."

The PM's words were sharp. He was upset about this unnecessary controversy. Yet, I could see that he trusted me. Otherwise things would have gone down differently in the meeting we'd just had. I left the PM's residence feeling guilty and confused. Had I let my leader down?

That evening, Zaira and I had a quick conversation over the phone. It wasn't just me the media was hounding. Quite a few of them had appeared outside the gates of her university as well, but the university administration had been understanding enough and had issued instructions to the guards to deny all of them entry. So far, keeping a low profile had helped Zaira keep the media at bay.

Tia had called me as well, worried about the media storm I was caught in. I reassured her and told her that I'd talk to her about everything once things quietened down a little.

But the problem with news channels these days is that they act like eagles hunting for prey. And hence, what had been reported as a scoop by one newspaper became a staple item on the news menu on national television over the next few days. They kept circulating stories of my involvement with a separatist leader's daughter ad nauseam.

One channel even had the obnoxiousness to obliquely

Chapter Eight: New Delhi, February 2017

suggest that I was on the payroll of Pakistan's ISI. Yet another absurdly suggested a CIA connection where Zaira and I were working on an alternate Kashmir agenda since Zaira was estranged from her father. The speculations were simply ludicrous.

The farrago of all the negative stories planted about me in the media was bound to impact public perception about the party and me. Three days later, this became evident to me in a core group meeting called by the PM, at the behest of Ratnakar Singh, the party president.

"The writing on the wall is pretty clear. If we are to win the impending State Assembly elections, we have to make some sacrifices . . ." Ratnakar Singh pointed out, looking directly at me.

"But asking Vihaan to go might seem like an acceptance of guilt on our part. Rather, we should stand by him," averred the finance minister, Anurag Gehlot.

"I think it's outrageously irresponsible for the defence minister to be involved with the daughter of a separatist leader. And this association goes back thirteen years, that's since before Vihaan entered politics. I would say it calls for a detailed investigation into Vihaan's conduct," Siddharth Gupta, the home minister, my rival for reasons known only to him, was at his acerbic best.

"Besides, attacks from Pakistan have increased lately. I am not sure whether it's the defence minister's distraction or what, but we have to act now . . ." the party president chipped in, making his dislike for me pretty obvious.

I wasn't unprepared for this assault. So I got up, took out an envelope from my kurta pocket, walked up to the PM, and held it out in front of him.

"What is this?" he queried.

"My resignation letter, sir. As I had told you in our last meeting, I stand committed to protecting our country's interests till my last breath. I wish to quit office till I prove myself innocent."

The PM nodded. "I trust you, Vihaan. But this resignation is important at this point."

My resignation had been accepted.

That evening, after two years of leading an extremely hectic life crowded with people, I was suddenly left alone to battle the biggest war of my life. My house was unusually quiet. The usual stream of visitors was conspicuous by its absence.

Zaira called me in the evening, concerned. When I told her about my resignation she wanted to come over and meet me, but I asked her not to, promising to meet her soon. I wanted some time alone to think things through inside my own head. I called Tia after that and told her about the resignation as well. She didn't say much, sensing my need to mull over things, and simply told me to take care and have my meals on time.

That night I felt incredibly restless, like I have felt very rarely in my life. The fear of losing things which I held so dear kept me jittery as the hours slowly ticked by. On the one hand, my political career was on the edge, and on the other, it seemed like I was about to lose my love again. But most importantly, it was the insinuation of being a 'traitor' that kept haunting me.

I had really fought my destiny to grab my pie of successes from life. But now, suddenly everything that belonged to me, was at stake. I couldn't just let it all go. I had to fight back and make sure I held on to every bit that belonged to me.

I stepped out into the verandah. To my surprise, it was raining. Perhaps even the Gods above felt some sympathy for

Chapter Eight: New Delhi, February 2017

me. Unable to calm myself, at about 1:30 a.m., I took my car out, and specifically instructing my security not to follow me, drove all the way to Zaira's university campus on the outskirts of Gurgaon. It took me about an hour to get there. It was an impulsive thing to have done and I was well aware of the possible futility of my action. Yet, I was prepared to fail rather than to let go without even trying.

Thankfully, the security guard at the campus gate recognised me—after all, my photograph had been splashed all over the media over the last few days. When I explained that I needed to talk to Zaira urgently, he opened the gate and proceeded to escort me right up to Zaira's quarter. I rang Zaira's doorbell a couple of times before she opened the door, rubbing her eyes, having been woken up from her sleep. She was stunned to see me there. I hugged her then, at her door step, and broke down.

Half an hour later, as we sipped the coffee Zaira had made, I found myself a little more composed and calm than what I had been. We were also in the middle of our most decisive conversation ever.

"Are you sure you want me to be with you?" asked Zaira, staring at me. "I mean I feel we are better off away from each other . . . my presence around you, it doesn't seem to do you much good . . ."

"Zaira—"

"No, Vihaan . . . let me finish . . . look at what's happening now. You've worked so hard to get here, but right after you met me again, after all these years, you've landed yourself in the biggest mess of your career, isn't it? Maybe I should just go away, forever . . ."

"I have always been very clear about what I want, Zaira. I

want you to stay with me. Forever. Now you have to make up your mind."

Zaira looked away, her dilemmas pretty apparent on her face. Then quietly, after a long moment, she put her hand over mine, holding it tightly, and nodded slightly.

"Let me go to Kashmir as planned. My presence in your house right now will not let you live in peace," she said.

"It's the fear of your absence that doesn't let me be in peace."

***

For the first time now, after having known each other for twenty-seven years, Zaira and I finally experienced what both of us had silently always craved for: living together under one roof. Although it was for just a week, since Zaira was still firm about leaving for Kashmir as she had originally planned, I hoped that she would change her mind at the end of the week. Every day, I'd wake up before her and prepare breakfast for the two of us before she left for work. I'd be caught all day in my study after that, making notes, strategising my next move, and meeting the few people who were still ready to support me. Zaira would return from work late in the evening. We'd sit together and discuss our respective days over cups of coffee or green tea. Later, we would have our dinner in the garden in the pleasant evenings of a Delhi spring.

I could see Zaira was worried for me and that she wanted to help me resurrect my political career. We would often engage in political discussions and try to brainstorm for a way out for me. We both also wanted to do our bit in trying to find a solution for Kashmir, where with every passing day the situation just

Chapter Eight: New Delhi, February 2017

seemed to be getting worse. The valley had reported the longest spell of curfew ever. It was no longer just a political problem. The people of the valley seemed to have been brainwashed by radical Wahabi and Salafi Islamic influences. Needless to say, the entire situation was being exploited by Pakistan, leading to an alarming increase in incidents of violence and attacks on our armed forces.

In almost all the reports of violence that kept pouring in from Kashmir, the name of Zaira's father kept popping up. It was suspected that Bilal Bhat was the *hawala* link in all these instances of Pakistan-sponsored violence.

Every time this happened, it naturally led to an awkward silence between Zaira and me.

"I still cannot believe that Uncle has reduced himself to this," I remarked one day.

Zaira took a deep breath and told me what she knew. "From what I found out, it appears that around 2009, Dad was in a big financial mess, thanks to some foolish business deals he had landed himself in. Things were so bad that he was on the verge of selling off our bungalow. That's when his brother-in-law, Noor's brother, got someone to bail him out by giving him a huge cash loan. It was only much later that Dad learnt that the funds had come directly from Pakistan's ISI. By then, however, he found himself trapped. I am not sure whether he voluntarily toed the Pakistan line after that or he was forced to, but that's how things have come to this point . . ."

I nodded. Zaira's explanation was irrelevant now. The situation that I was in was too ruthless to accept a simplistic explanation of bad timing and misfortune.

Time flew in the week that Zaira and I had together. Zaira was to fly to Kashmir on Saturday morning and Tia was to come back from her boarding school for the weekend on Friday. I dreaded how she'd react to Zaira's presence in the house even though I had told her about Zaira and what she meant to me.

"I've told you everything as a friend, *beta*. I hope you will understand my perspective and not be judgmental," is how I ended our conversation.

Tia didn't say much after hearing about Zaira. "We'll discuss this when we meet on Friday," is all she said.

When Tia and Zaira finally met, I literally had goosebumps in anticipation of how Tia would respond. It was okay for the world to ridicule my conduct and criticise my actions because I didn't really care about it, but I really dreaded Tia doing the same. And Zaira and Tia anyway had just one evening together as Zaira was to fly out the next morning. I felt tense as I introduced the two to each other. But I needn't have worried. While Tia was initially a little wary around Zaira, as the evening progressed and the two of them talked to each other, Tia seemed to warm up to Zaira. Perhaps the depth of our love was apparent to her, because as we were winding up for the night, she turned to me and said, "Dad, I'm so happy for both of you. Seldom does life offer a second chance, or in your case, a third chance . . . just grab it without thinking, Dad. There's a reason why you've met this time . . ."

I hugged Tia. I couldn't quite believe that my little girl had grown up so much, that she could accept this part of my life with such understanding. Overwhelmed, I pulled Zaira into my embrace as well, completing my world.

"Zaira, stay back, please. Don't go . . ." I mumbled into her ear.

Before she could respond, however, my personal security officer came rushing in.

Chapter Eight: New Delhi, February 2017

"What happened?" I asked, worried about the anxious look on his face.

"A news channel has created ruckus at the gate, sir. I think you need to intervene before things really get out of hand."

It turned out that reporters from Wired TV, a news channel that specialised in sleazy and scandalous reporting, had speculated that the "family get-together at former defence minister, Vihaan Shastri's house included separatist leader, Bilal Bhat, and two other unknown separatists from Kashmir." Upon being denied permission to barge in, the news channel had resorted to making wild allegations about my staff and was also threatening them bodily harm.

I was aghast. Not that I had expected high standards of ethics from the media, but what I was seeing in front of me was the worst form of yellow journalism. Incensed beyond reason, I stepped out to the gate and lashed out at the news channel team.

"Yes I'm having a family get-together with my old friend and daughter. But that's it. It's a Saturday evening and you low life creatures, you need to get lost!" I yelled in anger.

The men left, but only after taking about a hundred pictures of me screaming at them. As I turned around to go back inside, I found Zaira right behind me. Her expression said it all. I could see she felt guilty for having landed me in trouble yet again. I held her hand, trying to convey to her that it didn't really matter, but the fragile tranquillity of the evening had been shattered.

Early next morning, when I saw Zaira off at the airport, I felt an emptiness begin to gnaw my insides.

"Don't worry, Vihaan. Destiny can't keep us away for long," Zaira said, sounding brave.

"Then why are you leaving?"

"My absence will help you get over this crisis sooner, you know that..."

She kissed me then, in public, unconcerned about the people around. For me, the kiss was, in a way, the start of a rebellion I had no option but to embark upon.

That evening, Tia and I went out on a long drive. We talked intermittently, allowing ourselves long spells of silence.

"Dad, how do you see yourself getting out of this mess?"

I remained mum, lost in myriad thoughts.

"I'll tell you what I think?" Tia asked, holding my hand reassuringly, appearing much older than the sixteen-year-old kid she still was.

I heard her out and to my surprise, what she had in mind wasn't very different from what I had been contemplating for the past couple of days.

"Dad, it will be a huge gamble and only someone as brave as you can pull it off... I know you will," she said confidently.

Tia's confidence in me made me feel more capable than I had ever thought myself to be. Two days later, I addressed a packed press conference at the Press Club, with Tia by my side.

"I have decided to spend the next six months in the remote districts of Kashmir. I will do everything possible, everything within my means, to find a lasting solution to the problems which have caused immeasurable misery to many generations of people in the valley and have, quite literally, torn it apart. Kashmir is a ticking bomb and if we don't fix the problem now it might just be too late. Those are our people there and we cannot forsake them. I might fail in my endeavour but I owe it to my country to at least try.

Chapter Eight: New Delhi, February 2017

"Is this Kashmir yatra just a cover up for you to romance Zaira Bhat freely?" asked one journalist the moment I finished, trivialising my announcement with his cheap query.

Even as my blood boiled at this comment, I kept myself calm. "Well, there's no rule that says that you need to deprive yourself on the personal front in order to serve your country better. I love my country and nothing can come in the way of it. But what I do in my personal time is not a matter under discussion."

My press conference, as I had expected, created waves. I had committed myself to doing what no Indian politician had done so far—spending the next many months assessing the situation on ground, in Kashmir. To be honest, deep inside I feared the worst in as much as I hoped for the best. But life hadn't left me with too many options to choose from and playing it safe was definitely not something I could afford anymore. I had already sought approval from the PM, and although he hadn't been entirely convinced about my proposed Kashmir yatra, he had given me a go ahead.

As Tia and I had our dinner together on the eve of my departure for Kashmir, we were conscious of an extremely fluid future staring at us, of there being no certainty when, and if, we'd ever sit together and share a meal like this again.

PART FOUR

VIHAAN: KASHMIRIYAT, JAMHOORIYAT, INSANIYAT ... HINDUSTANIYAT!

CHAPTER NINE

Srinagar, March 2017

The Kashmir of 2017, where a section of its people unabashedly indulged in stone-pelting men of the Indian army, violates the rich history of the land and its distinct spirit of Kashmiriyat, as they call it. It's a travesty of fate and Kashmir's sheer misfortune that the land of Sufi saints was now negotiating the influence of Salafi and Wahabi thugs. In fact, on the day I landed in Srinagar, three days after my epochal press conference in Delhi, most parts of the city were under a curfew due to sporadic incidents of student violence across the valley.

In the last two and half years, as the defence minister, whenever I had to deal with Kashmir, there were three questions whose answers I always tried to find but couldn't quite get: Who is the Kashmiri youth's anger directed at? What is the future they see for themselves? Who is responsible for the mess that Kashmir is today? I hoped this time round that by spending time with the people in Kashmir, by living among them, and talking to them at length, I would be able to make some headway in finding the answers to these questions.

As my flight landed, the eternal optimist in me was quietly hoping that Zaira would meet me at the airport, even though I knew that we'd be better off if she didn't. My decision to travel to Kashmir had taken Zaira by surprise. She'd never thought I would embark upon such an adventure. We had spoken several times on the phone since the press conference and even as my plans for Kashmir crystallised, I think I managed to make her see some merit in the whole idea.

When I got out of the airport I found Masood, one of the party workers in the state, waiting outside to receive me. Masood was the owner of an Apple store in the heart of Lal Chowk and he had been kind enough to have me stay in his house for the entire duration of my Kashmir yatra. As I sat down for dinner with Masood's family—his four-year-old twin boys and his pretty homemaker wife—the conversation, quite naturally, revolved around my present trip.

"The situation is particularly grim this time. In the '90s, there were gun-toting militants. Now there are very few guns. But almost everybody is ready to pick up the stone," Masood rued the situation.

"Hmm . . ." I nodded. "Do you know where exactly is Bilal Mohammed Bhat hiding?" I asked Masood the next moment, my personal interest in it obvious.

"I have heard that he operates out of a hideout in a farmhouse in Kulgam. He doesn't want to be too visible since he is on the radar of the security forces . . ."

"Yes, I know. It appears that he is the kingpin of a fake currency notes racket which circulates this money to fund the violence. That's what our intelligence tells us."

"Then why don't you arrest him?" Masood almost seemed to challenge me.

Chapter Nine: Srinagar, March 2017

"We will, very soon. We've cut off the circulation network as much as we could. But his influence still runs very deep . . . It will take a bit of time to nab him."

I was aware that I didn't sound very convincing. But then internal security was not my department and I have no qualms about admitting that I wasn't particularly in the know about the home minister's strategy on Kashmir.

***

The next morning, when I took the two-hour picturesque drive to the hill town of Shopian, I could sense an uneasy calm all around me. There weren't any happy, smiling faces to be seen on the highway. What I saw instead were people who were fearful of when the next bout of violence would break out. When I entered the main market of Shopian, the police convoy I had been forced to accept by the state government following my car, I could see a surprised look on the faces of most people as I got out of the car. They couldn't seem to be able to imagine that the former defence minister would drive himself to their town without the full fanfare of security and media and then want to talk to them. A small section of youngsters were abusive and hurled invectives upon me, invariably linking them to my being a Hindu nationalist. But thankfully, a few elderly gentlemen intervened just then and shooed the boys away. One of the gentlemen, Masood told me, was the president of Shopian's traders' association, Wajibullah Shaikh. It was him that I was to meet in Shopian. He was my first contact.

"*As-salaam-alaikum*, huzoor," Wajibullah Shaikh greeted me. "What brings you here?" he asked.

"Your pain," I answered with a straight face, taking him aback.

An hour later, we sat over lunch at the residence of Wajibullah Shaikh, talking about what was happening in the valley.

"The violence which you see today is very different from the one that had gripped Kashmir in the 1990s. It's become a mass movement led by the youth and they, impressionable as youngsters are, are only too keen to revolt. In the 1990s, there was disappointment, today there is hatred," Wajibullah explained the situation. "For three decades now, Kashmir has lived under the shadows of militant extremism and the resultant army excesses to combat it. So the average youth of today has grown up being as familiar with violence as with education. The fact that cinema halls don't operate in Kashmir and sports' facilities are modest, leaves them with very little scope for entertainment. They don't really have any avenues where they can expend their energies. The vacuum makes them an easy prey to the absurd temptations of martyrdom and a delusional *azaadi* that is dangled in front of them."

I could feel a strong sense of personal loss in Wajibullah's tone. The cause of it revealed itself within moments.

"My son, Ghulam, has been gone for more than eighteen months now . . . he came in contact with Burhan Wani on the Internet and was brainwashed into picking up arms. Every day those men would send him ghastly videos of army excesses, many of which were doctored, and he'd shut himself in his room and watch them. We all knew what was happening. But the influence of those men was so strong that we couldn't do a thing about it. Our own son wouldn't listen to us. He blamed people like us, with our cowardice, for what was happening in the valley. We needed to take a stand, he said. He hardly spoke to us and hardly stayed at home. Then about a year and a half ago, he just disappeared. I went to his room in the morning to wake him up and found that his bed hadn't been slept in. I knew immediately that something was off. I opened his cupboard and saw that some of his clothes were gone, as was some money from his mother's purse.

"He called us a couple of days later and told us not to worry, that he was fine and among friends. But before we could ask him anything he cut the call. Ghulam would occasionally call us, each time from a different number. We knew we had lost him, still, every time we spoke to him we pleaded with him to come home, but he told us he would not rest in peace till the 'mission' was accomplished. But after Burhan's death he stopped calling altogether. He probably thought all his calls were being traced. I don't know if they were . . . As for us, we don't know where he is, not even if he's alive."

Wajibullah had tears trickling down his cheeks as he finished the story. His wife, who had been standing close by, broke down and quickly went inside. I couldn't imagine the pain they both must have been in, not knowing how or where their son was, or if he was still alive. I couldn't even think of imagining myself in a position where I wouldn't know where Tia was or how she was.

"Wajibullah ji, I-I-I am sorry," I said, putting my hand on his shoulder. "What do you want?" I asked him helplessly. "What can I do for you?"

"We are fine the way we are, Vihaan sahib, because what we want might never happen. I want the valley to go back in time to the 1970s, when there was a reasonable semblance of sanity here, when the fringe was still the fringe. But that can't be. We know that in all probability our son is never coming back to us alive. We also know how untrustworthy Pakistan is. The azaadi that these young boys are screaming and fighting for, that freedom could have been possible seventy years ago. But today we have simply walked into a tunnel with a dead end."

Wajibullah Shaikh was clearly a practical man and what he said made a lot of sense. But what his story couldn't hide was the stark truth about Kashmir in 2017: that there was very little connection between the two generations in most Kashmiri families. The youngsters who were baying for blood were not just revolting against India, but more so against the local Kashmiri leadership which had failed them consistently for the last seventy years.

Sad as it was, the rest of India and Kashmir had moved in opposite directions in the last three decades. Just as India liberalised the economy and embraced globalisation, Kashmir went back in time under radical Islamic influences which brought it closer to a culture of medieval bigotry instead of making it a part of India's foray into being a superpower. And while the older generation of Kashmiris today were more in sync with the temperament of a progressive, peaceful idea, the younger generation was closer to the philosophy of a radical, retrograde Islamic state, thus making the disconnect between the two generations virtually insurmountable.

***

Later that afternoon, we were taken by one of Wajibullah's men to a house where Ashfaq Wani, the district president of the ruling party of the state, was hiding. It was a rather dilapidated, single storey structure, guarded by no less than a dozen armed

Chapter Nine: Srinagar, March 2017

security guards. One of the guards frisked us before leading us into a small but cosy and technically well-equipped room.

Ashfaq, a man in his late thirties, was watching one of India's decidedly patriotic news channels and seemed to be in a terrible mood. The news channel was repeatedly playing out a video clip of a BSF jawan being kicked by some Kashmiri youth.

"See for yourself how your news channels manufacture hatred against the valley people?" he charged at me without even exchanging courtesies.

"So do you support a BSF jawan being kicked in that manner?" I countered.

"I can show you hundreds of videos of how our people have been brutalised by your army." The man then turned to his phone and actually played a couple of videos of some army men torturing a woman in Baramulla. "These are genuine video clips, Vihaan sahib, and they are very recent," he claimed.

"*Dekhiye* Ashfaq sahib, I don't claim to understand your pain in entirety but I want to. I want to understand the root cause of what is happening in Kashmir. That's the reason I am here. But you will have to understand that two wrongs don't make a right," I tried taking charge of the discussion.

"No. You don't. You don't understand anything at all, least of all our pain," Ashfaq shot back, beginning to look angry.

"Then make me understand," said I, unfazed.

***

Half an hour later, perhaps realising that I was indeed well-intentioned, Ashfaq had begun to open up.

"See Vihaan sahib, when your party and mine got together to form the government two years ago, people had a lot of hopes.

They had expected the government to carry forward Vajpayee's peace process and talk to all the stake-holders in the process. But this never happened. You have to accept that a good chunk of our party is pro-separatists. So when we couldn't ensure full participation in the peace talks they all turned against us. They accused us of cheating them," Ashfaq explained. "Besides, the situation has become particularly bad after the killing of Burhan Wani and the use of these pellet guns by the army. The sheer number of youth blinded by pellet guns has left a trail of rage that will destroy Kashmir," he warned.

"But how else would the Indian army have dealt with the stone-pelters? By dropping a bomb on them? They were civilians!" I confronted him.

"That might have actually been better. Death is any day better than what our lives have been reduced to," he argued. "The people of Kashmir don't trust us anymore. Things would have been different if your PM had started a dialogue with the separatists. But that never happened and look at us now. Me and at least half of my party leadership are under threat. Why else do you think I live like this? In hiding?"

I didn't want to question Ashfaq anymore, given the mental agony he seemed to be constantly battling, but the fact that an important member of the ruling party of the state should sound this despondent was an apt indication of just how doomed the situation was.

As I drove back to Srinagar a little later, in as much as my interactions with Wajibullah and Ashfaq played out in my mind, I was equally distracted by thoughts of Zaira. I couldn't wait to finally meet her.

Zaira was staying alone in one part of her father's bungalow in Nishat. While her father had gone underground in the last year, his second wife, Noor, and their son lived in another part of the bungalow. Zaira had minimal interaction with them.

It was dusk by the time I reached Zaira's bungalow. I saw her from behind, dressed in all white, sitting and working on her laptop on a workstation created right in the midst of the serene garden. The Dal was visible a little in the distance, beyond the boundary walls of the compound. The whole image, I felt, could've given the world's best photograph a tough competition.

"Zaira!" I called from behind.

"Come, Vihaan! I've been waiting for you," she said without turning around.

I went up to her and hugged her tightly from behind.

"Why didn't you come to the airport yesterday? And you didn't call or message throughout the day either!"

Zaira looked at me, her eyes a little sad. "I know we are together all the time and yet, being seen together won't let us be together . . . It will add to your problems."

"Hmmm . . . I know." There was such a clear demarcation between how our hearts felt and how our minds were expected to behave. I was glad we were able to retain this maturity even in these trying times.

We spent the rest of the evening together. I was to travel to Baramulla the next morning and when we started talking about the plan, Zaira suddenly looked a little anxious.

"Can I travel with you?" she asked me.

I was tempted to nod. I wanted her by my side at all times. But instead I shook my head because I feared for her safety. I knew that it was her apprehensions concerning my safety that made her want to travel with me, but these were apprehensions I couldn't assuage. There was a perpetual risk involved in my being in Kashmir and it was a fact that both of us had to accept.

She nodded and clasped my hand. How I wished we could be together all the time without us bothering the world or the world bothering us, just two ordinary people in love, watching the sun set over the Dal.

***

The next day as I travelled to the border town of Baramulla with Masood, the driver of our car narrated an unusual story of selfless courage shown by the people of Baramulla way back in October 1947. Apparently, Pakistani tribesmen had invaded the valley on 22 October 1947. When they reached the town of Baramulla after ransacking Muzaffarabad and Uri, however, they faced stiff resistance from the local population. Leading this local resistance was a young boy of nineteen, Maqbool Sherwani, who kept the raiders back by warning them that the Indian forces had arrived on the outskirts of the town. This piece of information was actually wrong—the Indian troops hadn't even landed in Srinagar until then—but it held back the raiders for a few crucial days. Of course Maqbool was soon found out, captured, tortured, nailed to a wooden cross, and shot repeatedly by the raiders. But the tale of his bravery survives to this day.

"But there is another Maqbool in Baramulla, sir, Maqbool Bukhari," the driver continued, shaking his head, "and what he did in April this year is probably making the original Maqbool turn in his grave! Maqbool Bukhari, a twenty-year-old, used his room in the government house provided to his father, a policeman, to set up a cyber-cell which was connected to a good thirty-eight districts of Pakistan, apart from the ones in the valley. He was part of some twenty-five Whatsapp groups, each

Chapter Nine: Srinagar, March 2017

with about two-hundred-plus members, half from across the border and half from the valley. These Whatsaap groups directly connected the stone-pelters and the wannabe Indian terrorists to their ideological gurus and sponsors across the border. When the Indian intelligence agencies busted this module, Maqbool fled overnight. In all likelihood, he had crossed over the LOC and was perhaps being groomed for larger chaos. Or for all we know, he might have been killed by his bosses."

"Is Maqbool's family still around in Baramulla?" I asked the driver.

"Yes, sir. His father still lives in the same house. What else can he do? It's not so easy to uproot an entire family and relocate somewhere else . . ."

"Hmm . . ." I turned to Masood then. "Masood, do you think it will be possible to find Maqbool's father and have a chat with him?"

"I can take you to him, sir," the driver interrupted before Maqbool could respond to my question. "I know him well enough . . ."

"That's settled then," I said. "We'll go see Maqbool's father first."

When I met Eijaz Bukhari, Maqbool's father, about an hour and a half later, I could see how the burden of what his son had done weighed heavily on him. His face was drawn and heavily marked with lines.

"Sahib, sometimes I just feel like killing myself, but who will look after my family after me? Nobody can deny that the youngsters in Kashmir have grown up seeing army excesses. But then the army has never harmed an innocent either . . . These youngsters think that the Indian army is their enemy, but we, we still believe that our enemy is Pakistan. If my son had stayed in India he would have been tried as per the law, but now I am not sure if he will return alive."

I asked Eijaz then if he would be willing to record a video message for similarly affected young people and their parents, recounting his personal experience and exhorting them to shun militancy.

Eijaz thought for a moment before replying. "I'm sorry. I can't do that," he said. "Nowadays our people have started targeting policemen's homes as well . . . If I do such a thing they'd surely attack my family, especially my two younger children."

I nodded, understanding Eijaz's predicament. I just put my hand on his shoulder reassuringly and left.

I spent the next couple of hours meeting a cross section of people in Baramulla. From government school teachers to doctors and shopkeepers, I talked to as many people as I could to get a real sense, an unprejudiced view of how things stood in reality. By the end of the afternoon as we made our way back to the car to return to Srinagar, I realised that first-hand interactions such as these, with people who were victims of the violence, were an eye-opener for an outsider like me. No amount of research or official meetings could give one a glimpse of the truth on ground. Perhaps that was what I needed to do, go on an extensive tour of Kashmir and reach out to its people in the deepest and remotest of corners. A cross-Kashmir yatra of sorts.

It was a while later that I finally remembered to take out my cell phone and check for missed calls and messages. That's when I saw there were some fifteen missed calls from Zaira. I had probably been in a no network zone when she'd called because my phone definitely hadn't rung that many times during the day. I called Zaira back immediately.

Chapter Nine: Srinagar, March 2017

"Vihaan! Are you all right?" Zaira picked up the phone on the first ring itself. She was virtually panting for breath.

"Yeah Zaira. I am absolutely fine, just heading back from Baramulla. Why, what happened?"

"Thank God! I was really scared. There was a news report that an army vehicle travelling to Baramulla had been put on fire. And I thought it was you . . ."

I had no clue about this incident. "Listen, I am absolutely fine. I should be in Srinagar in another hour and a half I think. I'll head straight to your house, okay? Masood can come back and pick me up later. Just cook something for dinner . . . I am famished." I didn't quite trust Zaira's cooking abilities but I figured the onerous task would prevent her from worrying.

"All right . . . I'll see you then," she said, still sounding shaken.

When I reached Zaira's house, she hugged me hard and did not let go of me for the next ten minutes.

"I-I-I thought I'd lost you . . ." she whispered brokenly, looking into my eyes.

"And I have lived with that fear all through," I said, tightening my embrace.

***

The next morning, Masood and I came to pick up Zaira to go and meet her father. Of the many things I had to settle, an important one was to try and make Bilal Bhat see reason. I knew it was an improbable task, nonetheless, not attempting it was not an option. And when Masood had told me that he knew Bilal's hideout—as did almost everyone else in Srinagar—I had been surprised. From what I gathered, when someone went 'absconding' in Kashmir, often this version was for the consumption of the Indian establishment. Local Kashmiris showed empathy for their people and invariably knew the hideouts of these 'absconders'.

The nearly one-and-a-half-hour journey along a highway dotted on both sides by beautiful mountains and lush green fields was a rather strained and tense one. I knew Zaira was really nervous, after all she would be meeting her father after a good seven years or so, and in conditions she couldn't have ever imagined possible.

When we entered the lavish and perfectly hidden farmhouse about two kilometres off the highway, it was like entering an eerie den. It was silent, dark, and cold like a tomb. We were led in from one room to the other, completing messing up our sense of direction, until we finally reached a room where we saw an aged man bent over a rug, offering *namaaz*. It was Bilal. All over the room, there were religious books strewn across. A particularly strong smell of *ittar* seemed to permeate every corner of the room. I found it difficult to believe that the man sitting with his back towards us was the same suave man I had first met in a five star hotel in Delhi and then in his own house in Srinagar, in very different conditions.

We waited quietly until Bilal finished his prayers. When he opened his eyes and saw his daughter standing right in front of him, his face literally crumpled up and his eyes became moist. He silently opened his arms for Zaira and she ran to him.

"Dad, I've come to take you back," Zaira told him authoritatively.

But Bilal looked around ruminatively and then smiled. "Unfortunately Zaira, I've reached a point where there are no roads going back. Death for me might be closer than azaadi."

Chapter Nine: Srinagar, March 2017

"Uncle, let the kids romance this delusion of independence. People like you are better off doing a reality check," I kind of admonished him, surprising myself.

"What reality check are you talking about?" Bilal demanded, enraged with what I had said. "The reality that we were fooled into being a part of India and then cheated repeatedly as India went back on her promise of plebiscite? And that now after seventy years, we have no option but to either accept India's rule or face her bullets? Is that what you want me to accept?"

Zaira tried calming him down but I didn't feel like letting him get away with this trademark gibberish.

"Uncle, our intelligence reports clearly tell us that you had always denounced the Hurriyat leaders. It was only when you became bankrupt, thanks to some bad business deals, that your brother-in-law got you some ISI money and bailed you out. You didn't know about all this until much later, didn't you? They set up a new business for you—flooding the economy of Kashmir with fake currency notes and using those to buy weapons. You are directly funded by the ISI. You never had an ideology. You fell victim to that, plain and simple."

Bilal looked at me long and hard, as if assessing me. Then he shrugged his shoulders. "Yes, this is what I am, a victim," he said. "And this is what the azaadi movement today has been reduced to. And I blame India for this. It is people like you, sitting up there in the centre, thinking you know what is best for us, who have brought this calamity upon us. It is you who have left us with nowhere to go."

I realised there was nothing really that I could say to Bilal to make him change his mind. I watched Zaira sit next to her father and talk to him about other, mundane things. I felt saddened by Bilal's condition. Here was a man who had successfully weathered many storms in life with prudence and aplomb, but today he seemed every bit a man who had lost everything—his home, his family, his life, his very independence. What, I wondered, could you possibly say to someone who was but a pawn in a larger game?

What I saw of Bilal here, of Wajibullah and Ashfaq in Shopian, and of Eijaz in Baramulla, brought home to me an inescapable truth: that the last three decades of militancy and mayhem in the valley had made people fight the worst forms of depression and mental agony.

After chatting alone with her father for a good half hour, Zaira joined me outside. I'd left them alone for some time.

"Let's go," she said, looking pensive.

"He won't see reason?"

"There are times when you've just got to leave things to destiny. He is not the father who raised me . . ."

***

That afternoon after returning to Srinagar, we met an independent MLA, Faraaz Lone, in a café in Lal Chowk. Faraaz had an interesting story. Coming from an educated family of well-known lawyers, Faraaz had left his profession to join the militants in the mid '90s. Within five years, when his bosses in Pakistan realised that he might not give in to Pakistan completely but instead, insist on independence, they tried killing him. Faraaz escaped by going underground. But his father was killed in broad daylight by some militants. This made Faraaz see through the evil designs of Pakistan. He shunned militancy and instead, joined mainstream politics to work at bringing about change in the valley. Faraaz had been in touch with my secretary ever since I had initiated my Kashmir plan, and I had been looking forward to meeting someone like him.

"Vihaan bhai, to be honest, we Kashmiris have seen it all from time to time. We have striven for independence, we have toyed with the idea of joining Pakistan, and we have also tried to make ourselves believe that our destiny lies with India," he explained.

"So where do you stand now?" I tried to understand.

"A majority of us would still want independence, but we are fine with India. Very few, however, trust Pakistan."

"Then why, rather how does Pakistan end up playing such a big role here?" I asked, confused.

"That's because the Indian establishment lets it do so. Invariably, when there is unrest in the valley, the Indian establishment tends to disown the whole of Kashmir. This is something which Kashmiris hate. Our slimy neighbour takes full advantage of the situation and like a lascivious suitor, offers all kinds of inducements. It's okay for India to completely ostracise Pakistan and cut off all ties with it, but never ever let your communication with the people of Kashmir break down. If we were that unfaithful we wouldn't have stayed with you for seventy years . . ."

Even after Faraaz was gone, his words echoed in our ears. Zaira and I had continued sitting in the café, sipping half a dozen cups of *kahwa* between us as the hours went by, hoping to make some progress in understanding the conundrum called Kashmir. I had told Zaira about my idea of the Kashmir yatra and while she agreed that it seemed to have some potential for turning things around, she was sceptical about the sort of reception I would get from the people. No other Indian leader from the centre had ever undertaken something like this in the valley and there was a huge security risk involved in the whole exercise. But the more I interacted with the locals, the more I realised that the issue was far more layered and complex than what it had appeared to be. I knew I really needed to expand the scope of my reach. The whole situation reminded me of some Shakespearean lines from the *Macbeth*: "Fair is foul and foul is fair: Hover through the fog and filthy air . . ."

"You still remember lines from your school books?" Zaira asked, laughing when I recited the lines for her.

"Yeah, some of them . . ."

"Come, I'll take you somewhere," she said, getting up suddenly and holding out her hand, excitement sparkling in her eyes.

Curious, I quickly paid the bill and followed her out. That evening, Zaira showed me around her school, Mallinson Girls. It was a beautiful heritage building with brick-coloured exteriors and raised green tops, a far cry from the sleek, steel and glass buildings that are the international schools that dominate the education sector today. I instantly fell in love with the place.

"That, there, is my first classroom," Zaira pointed out to a room as we walked through a corridor. "And that used to be our kindergarten classroom. Our class teacher used to be this chubby Christian lady, Miss Gabriel."

I could see a small smile on Zaira's face. Sometimes, nostalgia was a good thing. Walking around her school was a break we both needed after the intense engagements we had been dealing with all day.

"That's the volleyball court. I dabbled in volleyball for a couple of years until I lost interest in the game. And there's our auditorium where I participated in an elocution contest for the

Chapter Nine: Srinagar, March 2017

first time." Zaira was getting truly emotional. I felt happy to be able to have her relive some moments from her growing up years.

"Come, I'll take you to the adjoining boys' school, the Tyndale Biscoe."

When we entered Tyndale Biscoe, however, I could see an immediate change in Zaira, as if she were burdened by some painful memories. "What happened Zaira, are you all right?" I asked.

She nodded faintly. "Yash . . . he had proposed to me right here after our Socials meet. And just behind that wall, there, we shared our . . . ah, forget it!"

"Say it, Zaira . . ."

"Our first kiss . . ."

"You still remember him as much?" I asked her, touching her face.

"No . . ." she shook her head, "but this place, it reignites old memories."

"Hmmm . . ."

"Vihaan, let's go from here. I've had enough of nostalgia for one evening anyway."

I could see Zaira really wanted to get out of the place and it was quite dark anyway.

As we walked back along the Dal Lake, holding hands, I wanted to savour these moments with Zaira. I was not unaware of the risk I was taking in walking on near-empty roads without any security, but I didn't want to think about the political situation anymore. I didn't want to worry about what was going on in the valley or whether I was going to find any kind of a solution to the mess. On an impulse, I stopped and kissed Zaira. For a moment, it took her by surprise, but the very next instant she reciprocated. We gave in to each other, relishing the physical proximity that the cover of the dark night gave us.

"Does this feel better than your first kiss?" I asked her, surprised by my own possessiveness.

"Do you really expect an answer?" she smiled.

Just then my cell phone rang. It was Mahesh, my secretary from Delhi.

"Sir, are you all right?"

"Yes, I am fine, Mahesh. Why? Has something happened?"

"Yes sir. They're just breaking the news right now. A Kashmiri army officer, Umar Fayaz, who had gone to attend a relative's wedding in Shopian, has been brutally killed by some militants . . . the situation is just getting worse, sir. You need to be very careful . . ."

This was indeed bad. The killing had apparently taken place in the same area of Shopian which I had visited just two days ago. It was a step further towards the total chaos and havoc that was threatening the valley. With every passing day, it seemed to me that what little window the valley had of dispelling the darkness it was engulfed in, was shrinking.

CHAPTER TEN

Srinagar, March 2017

*Nationalism is power-hunger
tempered with self-deception*
– George Orwell

Zaira and I spent the whole of the next day making our way through over a hundred files with some five-hundred articles in all, in an attempt to understand the historical background of the problem in Kashmir. It was a marathon session, yes, but it helped me understand a little better the nuances of the issues at play in the valley.

Much of Kashmir's problems seemed to emanate from the basic fact that for a land area that big, there were far too many ethnic divisions within it. So while the Kashmir valley comprised largely of Kashmiri Muslims with a small percentage of Kashmiri Hindu Pandits; in Jammu, majority of the population comprised of Dogras. Ladakh was Buddhisht, while Gilgit and Balistan, now a part of Pakistan, had a majority population of Dardi and Balti tribes. The areas of Muzzafarabad and Mir, now part of POK, had a Punjabi-Muslim population, dissimilar from the valley-Muslims.

Putting so many different people together under one single administrative system was bound to be fraught with tension.

Over the years, as the political players in power kept changing, so did the nature of the politics that dominated the valley. So, from Hari Singh, the last Dogra ruler of Jammu and Kashmir, reluctantly agreeing to join India in October 1947, and the wily Sheikh Abdullah's hobnobbing with Pakistan to wrangle favours and concessions from the Indian government to Atal Bihari Vajpayee's slogan of *Kashmiriyat, Jamhooriyat, Insaniyat* that was a catch phrase for the three-pronged approach he had in mind to solve the Kashmir question, the dispute in Kashmir spiralled into a huge, complex jumble of a hundred different strands that now appear virtually impossible to untangle.

I felt completely spaced out and drained as I closed the last of the files. I had in fact, been battling a headache for the last hour or so. Zaira and I both decided to venture out of the house and walk around a bit. Perhaps the fresh air would do us good.

It was fairly dark when Zaira and I reached Lal Chowk, outside what was a stark reminder of Srinagar's happier past—the Palladium Cinema hall, the most famous cinema hall in the valley at one point in time. Sadly, after the advent of militancy, it had been shut down and was used later to shelter security forces.

We walked over to a small tea shop near the hall where, Ali, its septuagenarian owner greeted us with a big toothy grin.

"*As-salaam-alaikum!*"

"Salaam, Ali!" We greeted the man and sat down on the one rickety wooden bench that made up his shop. I asked for two cups of my favourite *kahwa* with saffron.

"You know, sahib," Ali started his usual chitchat as he poured out the tea, "in the '60s and '70s, this road used to be buzzing with people till well past midnight. And especially so if there was a hit movie playing at the Palladium . . . People would come out after the last show and have *kahwa* at my stall. I had a roaring business in those days . . . At times, I too, watched movies there with my begum. I remember seeing *Bobby*, *Sholay* and *Muqaddar Ka Sikandar* here, but then, as the radical forces grew in strength, all the good things around died . . ."

Every time a Kashmiri reminisced about his glorious past, it really hurt me. I just couldn't understand how a state could regress so much when the rest of the country progressed consistently. To an extent, it was perhaps okay to blame the complicated accession of Kashmir to India, but could one really absolve the local leaders of Kashmir of their non-performance, especially when the Indian government was so ready to pamper the state?

The half hour that Zaira and I ended up spending outside the Palladium, with Ali regaling us with one story after the other about how thriving and vibrant the place used to be, gave us an idea or two.

"If we want to really turn things around, it's the cinema and the arts that will have to play a crucial part," I told Zaira.

"But successive state governments have tried to reopen the cinema halls, twice in the last two decades to be exact. But they didn't succeed," she sounded a note of caution.

"Then they clearly have not tried hard enough. One has to be persistent; change doesn't come about overnight, does it? The state governments here, they've done nothing for the good of Kashmir," I responded, unable to hide my anger.

Later that night, we let go of the two police constables who were accompanying us as my security detail and decided to go on a shikara ride on the Dal Lake.

"Wow! I can't imagine we're doing this again," Zaira spoke quietly as our boatman ferried our shikara to the centre of the lake. It was a dark night with the moon just a sliver in the sky. There were just a couple of shikaras around. Essentially, it was just the two of us. It was perfect.

"We will experience many more things together, I promise you that. That motorcycle drive to Pahalgam is still pending," I smiled.

"Oh you remember that?"

"Of course. We have to make that happen . . ."

Three things happened simultaneously in the next instant: we heard a gun fire from somewhere close by, the bullet rending through the still night air, and our boatman fell down, shrieking in agony, rocking the shikara dangerously. It took me a moment to realise that someone had fired a gun in our direction and that it had hit our boatman. Then it struck me that this was probably an assassination attempt on me. My immediate thought was Zaira. I turned around to check on her and found her scrambling over to the boatman, his burly frame providing her with some sort of a cover.

That's when I heard the sound of oars splashing from somewhere nearby, but all I could make out was the dark shape of a small boat getting away. I couldn't make out its occupants.

With our boatman bleeding profusely, I rowed the boat back as fast as I could. Zaira had fashioned a rough tourniquet to keep the pressure on the wound, but the man needed urgent medical attention. She called Masood from my phone to inform him of what had happened, and thankfully, by the time we got to the lakeshore, he was already there to take us to the hospital.

What remained of the night was a haze. All I could think about, with my heart thumping loudly, was that the bullet that had hit the boatman could have hit Zaira. I had put her in danger. It was my being in Kashmir, doing what I was doing, which had put her in harm's way.

Sometime during the course of the night, with a reinforced police detail around us, we left the hospital. Masood reassured us that he would take care of things there and would keep us posted regularly. Zaira and I were absolutely quiet on the ride back home. But the minute we got home, Zaira turned to me, livid.

"Listen Vihaan, you have to stop this drama here!"

"Drama? You think this is all a drama?!" My fear for Zaira wasn't letting me think straight.

"I mean either you ask for Z+ security again, or you let me be with you all the time," she demanded, her insecurities and fears fairly obvious.

I took a moment to gather myself and then shook my head.

"Fine . . . then just don't involve me in any of your plans in the future!" she stormed away.

I followed Zaira, trying to reason with her, but in vain. I couldn't afford a heavy security cover because that would prevent me from reaching out to the average Kashmiri as a friend, as an ordinary man. I couldn't let Zaira come with me either because I couldn't risk losing her forever. I felt quite helpless negotiating the predicament I was in.

That very same day, a couple of hours after we got home, I got a call from the PM asking me to come and see him immediately.

***

I met the PM early next morning, having flown in from Srinagar the evening before. I had been flooded with calls after the assassination attempt made it to breaking news on prime-time television. The police were apparently already in hot pursuit of two young men who were the main suspects. No terror group had claimed responsibility of the attack, at least not yet. And while Zaira had refused to talk to me properly before I left, I couldn't not come to Delhi when the PM had personally asked me to.

"Is it going anywhere, your Kashmir project?" the PM asked me straightaway.

I nodded, not entirely sure how much I could share just yet. I had a fair idea of what I was going to do in the next three months, but my thoughts were largely in my head. I didn't have a blueprint ready the way the PM liked to see it. I also knew that in the big game-changer plan I had in mind, I would need the government's support at a very critical juncture. After some initial moments of hesitation, however, I went ahead and spelt out the plan to the PM—a twenty-three-day-long road yatra across the valley.

"Give me three months, sir. What I am planning to do is ambitious and unprecedented. There are more chances of failing than there are of succeeding, but if I do succeed, Kashmir will be a different story."

"You know Vihaan, ideally I should stop you. Because in my government, nothing happens without me approving of it. But somewhere in you, I see a younger me. I have been the rebel who has challenged status quo without the fear of failure. My instincts are telling me to let you do the same."

I heaved a huge sigh of relief. Did the PM really trust me so much? Or was it a unique win-win situation for him? Now

Chapter Ten: Srinagar, March 2017

that I was not a part of the government, if things went wrong I could easily be disowned completely. But if things went right, the PM could take full credit for the plan and for backing me up. Well, the PM was a well-intentioned manipulator and I wasn't complaining.

"But I have two conditions," the PM continued. "Three months is all you have, after which you will have to leave Kashmir. We can't risk losing you there."

I nodded. "What's the second condition, sir?"

"You will have the necessary security to guard you. I don't want any future attacks like last night's."

"But sir, a mass contact programme with the people in the interiors of Kashmir is what I had planned . . . it will be critical in executing what I have in mind. A heavy security detail will be an unnecessary deterrent. Besides, sir, I am not particularly scared about dying in Kashmir. You see, my father had unflinching faith in astrology and had shown my horoscope to almost every astrologer in Varanasi. All of them have predicted that I will live beyond eighty."

The PM laughed when he heard this. But he insisted on the security cover. In a way I was glad about it because it would anyway end my dilemma and put Zaira at ease. I tried calling her after the meeting got over but she didn't take my calls. I guess she was still upset with everything that had happened, and the speculations that were doing the rounds of the media were certainly not helping her calm down.

After coming out of the meeting with the PM, I went to meet an old journalist friend, Pranab Goswami. Pranab was an audacious nationalist and was forever ready to do anything for the country. I knew that in the scheme that was beginning to consolidate itself in my mind, the support of the media, or at least a section of it, was critical. When I proposed to Pranab what I had in mind for his news channel, he was more than happy to execute it for me. We spoke at length about the whole plan and his positive response, along with the PM's support, made me feel more determined than ever as I prepared myself mentally for a decisive stint in the valley.

CHAPTER ELEVEN

Srinagar, July 2017

The flag of Independent Kashmir was hoisted in Srinagar by Khalid Raza Burhani, the twenty-seven-year-old leader of the militant group Al-fateh-Kashmir, on 26th October 2021, exactly seventy-four years after Kashmir became a part of India. However, this newly formed outfit of rabid and violent youngsters who had virtually usurped the state in the last couple of years, had little in common beyond a pathological hatred for India and a psychotic love for establishing the rule of the Caliphate.

Within months of the formation of Independent Kashmir, cracks surfaced within Al-fateh-Kashmir. A splinter group, led by one Moruf Bhat, rebelled against Khalid, accusing him of being insincere to the tenets of 'real Islam'. This group owed direct allegiance to the ISIS. It went over to Syria for training and deliberations about the future of the valley. One year later, they resurfaced and unleashed unthinkable vengeance on Al-fateh-Kashmir, managing to wipe out a fair number of its members.

With the ISIS struggling to keep its hold on Syria and West Iraq intact, it found Kashmir to be a safer haven. With the help of Moruf Bhat's splinter group, ISIS overthrew Khalid and seized complete control of Kashmir. What followed was unprecedented brutality in the name of the Shariat. Khalid was hanged from a tree in downtown Srinagar, as were about five-hundred of his supporters. A large number of women from across the state were taken as sex slaves. What was meant to be a happy and prosperous Azaad Kashmir was reduced to being a slave state of the ISIS.

No, this wasn't real. This was a six-minute-long animation film made by Feroze Mattoo, a native of Kashmir, studying in an animation and graphics college in Delhi.

"The youth of Kashmir is so intoxicated with flimsy notions of azaadi that it needs a reality check. This film gives them that reality check," he explained.

Even as I mulled over the option of using the video, I wondered how, over the centuries, personal avarice had indeed concocted righteous motives to unleash the worst forms of bigotry. Aurangzeb was a glaring example of that side of Islam which ought to have been shunned after his death. Yet the meek Indian psyche allowed roads and towns to be named after him. No wonder he still begets like-minded bigots who believe in his form of religious anarchy, albeit with newer identities.

I had spent little more than five months in Kashmir now and one thing was abundantly clear to me: Kashmir was not a political problem alone, it was an outright problem of Islamic radicalisation. As such, any temporary move to solve the problem could not ignore the prospect of the larger danger resurfacing in future.

In this context, I am tempted to believe in India not having gone all out to renege POK and the Northern Parts way back in 1948. Perhaps a second line of thought which must have prevailed upon the Indian leadership was that since the division of the country was anyway on religious lines, to have those parts of Kashmir back in India might make it tougher

Chapter Eleven: Srinagar, July 2017

for India to retain them. Instead, the portion of Kashmir which India retained along with Jammu and Ladakh, seemed more manageable. Of course this is just an interpretation, and interpretations can never be accurate because those in decisive leadership positions carry their thoughts and secrets with them to their graves.

***

I woke up at around five in the morning with that particular consciousness that weighs heavily on the mind when you know you have an onerous task to execute. My proposed Kashmir yatra was just two days away now. The risks were high but if I succeeded, I knew it could be the game-changer for Kashmir that we needed. What was also bothering me was the slight strain that had crept into my relationship with Zaira. Even though I had spoken to her after coming back from Delhi and reassured her that upon the PM's insistence, I would keep my security cover from now, she had sounded a little distant. I knew I had to go and see her to sort things out, because unless I did that, I wouldn't be able to devote myself completely to the yatra. But I hadn't had a moment to spare since my return from Delhi. Every waking minute had been taken up in preparing for the yatra and ironing out all the logistical details. Mahesh, my secretary, had flown in from Delhi with me to help, but it was still a mammoth task.

Two hours later, determined to mend things between us before I did anything else, I stood outside Zaira's bungalow in the most unexpected of get-ups—a beard, a thick woollen cap, a helmet, and a pair of dark glasses. And yeah, I had Maqbool's Harley Davidson with me.

Half an hour later, after Zaira came to terms with my shocking, impulsive act, we were on our way to Pahalgam, and about four hours after that, we sat on the banks of River Lidder. Of course it was a risky thing to have done. But it couldn't have been any more suicidal than my Kashmir yatra. And I was willing to take the risk, especially when it came to Zaira, because I couldn't bear the thought of leaving even the smallest of her wishes unfulfilled.

So there we were, with our feet in the water and our hands clasped, soaking in the majestic serenity all around us, acutely aware that this could well be a once-in-a-lifetime experience, considering the uncertainty both of us were living with.

"You won't change ever, will you?" Zaira asked, smiling. "How did you plan all this?"

"Only your professional life can be planned," I replied. "The personal bits are all impulsive." But even as I said that, I wondered if it was that simple really.

Zaira kissed me then and I lost myself in the kiss.

We spent a long time after that in a virtual trance, just listening to the sound of the river flowing and being one with nature, like inseparable age-old lovers. There was no discussion about whether Zaira would accompany me on the yatra or not.

We drove back to Srinagar after lunch, having given ourselves a moment of simple happiness that both of us had so desperately been in need of.

***

The next day was a quiet, focussed one as I got down to reviewing every minute detail of the yatra. I had spent weeks planning things out but with so much at stake, I couldn't help worrying about the small details incessantly.

Chapter Eleven: Srinagar, July 2017

I found myself mulling over the larger approach I had to take and comparing Kashmir to an exceptionally gorgeous but equally strong-headed, independent-minded woman whom India loved. The two had their issues, like any two people in a relationship. Pakistan was the wily suitor and did everything it could to drive an irreparable wedge between Kashmir and India. Now if India had to win Kashmir over, it had to be through love and respect. India would have to create that sense of belonging which is critical in any relationship. And strange as it may sound, the rules of engagement, both in personal relationships and in political alliances are similar—it's all about developing a sense of trust, mutual respect, and belonging.

Day 1, Srinagar

The tallest point in Srinagar is the Adi Shankaracharya Temple of Lord Shiva. I wanted to start my Kashmir mission from here. The reason was simple: there are very few individuals as inspiring in Indian history as Adi Shankaracharya, the great 9th century Indian philosopher from Kerala, who had travelled across the length and breadth of the country and who is credited with unifying the various thoughts in Hindusim. I prayed to Lord Shiva to give me the strength of the great ancient philosopher to succeed in my own mission of unification. Zaira stood by my side, in obeisance. We looked much like a married couple, and we were conscious of the need to not be seen so.

Two hours later, I was all set to address my first public meeting at Lal Chowk, the heart of Srinagar and the venue of many an uprising planned and executed against India. To turn the narrative around, Lal Chowk had to become the venue of reintegration.

I had the option of requesting the local party members to flood my meeting, maybe even have some more members ferried from Jammu to swell the numbers. But that would have defeated the purpose. That would have made me resemble any other politician. I knew my mission would not succeed without actual local involvement, hence, with minimal support from my own party cadre, my secretary and I had gone ahead and arranged everything for the meeting. The state government had provided a police cordon around the area.

I waited with Zaira as people gathered slowly. Most were curious bystanders who wanted to know what was going on. I waited until a group of about fifty people had assembled. Then I got onto the makeshift stage and addressed them.

"Friends, the chaos and mayhem that Kashmir has intermittently witnessed in the last seven decades would shame any civilisation, more so ours which prides itself on culture and peace. I am not here to point fingers. I am not here to indulge in the blame game. I am here because Kashmir deserves better. Let's make a fresh start right here, right now—"

Barely had I said this when a group of over hundred young protestors barged into the meeting, shouting anti-India slogans and carrying flags of Pakistan. I could see the policemen immediately stiffen and ready themselves to open fire in warning. They would, I realised, retaliate with violence—firing pellets or lathi-charging the protestors. That was not what I wanted. An ugly incident like that would not only cause embarrassment to the government, it would also kill all my plans. But before the police could take on the protestors, Zaira quickly thought of a plan and whispered it in my ears.

"Please stop," I announced on the mike. "Let them shout

pro-Pakistan slogans. I will shout pro-India slogans. Let's see who can out-shout the other!"

For a moment the protestors were taken aback. They weren't prepared for this kind of an unconventional challenge. But the very next moment, they started shouting pro-Pakistan slogans with all their might, staring at me defiantly. My people, less than half in number, retaliated and began shouting "*Vandemataram*!" and "*Bharat Mata ki Jai*!" as loudly as they could. I wasn't one to be left behind either. Exploiting the advantage of the mike in front of me, I joined them, shouting as loudly as I could, my voice booming across Lal Chowk through the loudspeakers we had put up.

This amusing competition went on for about six to seven minutes before the army arrived on the scene and the protestors beat a hasty retreat.

As I watched the protestors leave Lal Chowk, I realised that slogans of *Bharat Mata ki Jai* were only getting louder with every passing minute. That's when I noticed that from the fifty-odd people we had at the start of the event, there were some two-hundred people shouting pro-India slogans now, and most of them were local people who had come of their own accord!

Day 5, Anantnag

Anantnag City is barely sixty kilometres southeast of Srinagar, falling on the way to Pahalgam. The road connecting Sringar to Anantnag, however, is in a pathetic state and it is quite an ordeal to drive to Anantnag. When you enter Bijbehara, the main town of the district of Anantag, it is easy to sense the frustration building up among the youth there. I almost felt as if it was a part of the very air there, being as it was a manifestation of perhaps a subconscious realisation that a bleak, fettered future was staring at them. Fettered because this generation of Kashmiris had grown up hating India and were forced to live within its boundaries. And bleak because even though the rest of India would embrace them with open arms, their own ego wouldn't easily let them accept the opportunities offered. And this 'forced unemployment' made them an easy prey to secessionist sentiments. In fact, so strong was the antagonism in Bijbehra that even though the only cricketer from Kashmir to play for India, Parvez Rasool, came from Bijbehara, he didn't enjoy even a fraction of the celebrity status which Burhan Wani did.

What Zaira and I had realised was that the violence in Kashmir wasn't driven from Srinagar anymore. It emanated from the interiors and the villages, places which had never been considered politically important. These were, therefore, the places where one had to be extra careful in striking the right chord with the people.

So Zaira and I spent a whole day visiting three remote villages of Anantnag district—Dachee Gam, Chandri Gam, and Chunda Pora. We tried to meet at least one family in each of these villages, which had lost a family member to violence in the last three decades.

What shook me everywhere was the absolute disconnect between two generations within a family. While the elders in the family wanted peace, they had no control over the younger generation. The younger generation on the other hand, was fed a regular diet of venom by groups operating at the behest of Pakistan, all in order to keep their anger and their sense of betrayal perpetually stoked. They were alienated not just from India but from their own families as well. A major percentage of them was also battling acute mental stress and depression.

Chapter Eleven: Srinagar, July 2017

Later that evening, I addressed a public gathering in the heart of Anantnag city. The number of people who had turned up to hear me was slightly better this time. There were about 150 people now. I guess they were showing their appreciation for me visiting their villages.

"Saab, even the local politicians have never done that," said one of those who had turned up to hear me.

Even as I was speaking to the people, I was interrupted by a middle-aged man who looked all dishevelled and was clearly in a bad shape. A local supporter informed me that he was a former militant who had surrendered and was now with India. His name was Yasin.

"Stop, Vihaan saab. Stop!" the man called out, surprising me. "What is it that you have to offer to us, huh?" he charged at me, making his way through the crowd.

"Jobs, roads, schools, a better life, respect . . ."

"Huh," he snorted. "That's a clichéd narrative . . . If you really want to help us, then protect us from the parasite called Pakistan."

Zaira and I were stunned when we heard this.

"That's the hard truth," Yasin continued. "In 1990, I came under the influence of Pakistani agents and crossed over to POK for an arms training course. Five years later, I realised they were a bunch of louts who could kill anybody for money. They were mercenaries and I wanted to leave them. When they found out that I wanted to escape, they shot me in my right eye. But somehow, I still managed to get away and come back home. They made ten more attempts to kill me, but each time Allah saved me. Then in 1999, I surrendered to the police. After spending a few years in jail, I was rehabilitated. Today, I run a small grocery store here. I have saved at least fifty children from falling for Pakistani propaganda and running away to become terrorists. I live in constant fear of being abducted and tortured and killed. But I will not let Pakistan waste the lives of other young people like they wasted mine. Not anymore. If you want to restore normalcy to the valley, then first show Pakistan its place. Keep it out of our affairs. Then see how most of the problems end in the valley."

I walked over and hugged Yasin when he finished. The cruelty and the experiences he had lived through in those five years in the training camp had left him a little mentally disturbed, but what he had said made sense. If the external player was removed from the entire mess, then there was a greater possibility of things getting simplified enough to be eventually resolved.

To my surprise, the crowd began to shout slogans of *India Zindabad* as we finished. I turned to Zaira and held her hand tightly in mine. For the first time, I felt a small glimmer of confidence that victory could well be within the realm of reality.

Day 12, Pulwana

A twenty-three-day yatra is always fraught with risks and in the situation that prevailed in Kashmir, it only made sense to take one day at a time. However, with each passing day, as we moved from one town and village to another, as we met more and more people, our confidence only grew. What also surprised me was how people were responding to Zaira's presence beside me. We hardly faced any censure anywhere and were met mostly with curiosity about the actual agenda of the yatra, not about the exact details of our relationship. Even the media didn't unnecessarily dramatise the fact that we were publicly presenting ourselves as a couple in spite of not being married to each other. Apart from a few articles in the initials days about Zaira and my relationship, the media focus shifted to the work we had set out to do. I suppose we were so absorbed with the purpose of the yatra that our feelings for each other were no longer the focus of our interactions. We were co-workers, plain and simple, and that must have become evident for everyone else around us too.

We were in Pulwana, where Zaira was to address the students at the women's college there. We hadn't been very optimistic about the number of students who would attend, but a good two-hundred girls had turned up.

Zaira began talking to the girls about her experiences as a girl from Kashmir, who was now a successful author and had travelled extensively throughout the world.

"When I was growing up in Srinagar some three decades ago," she said, "we had big dreams in our eyes. We had the calm confidence to take on the world. But today, when I look at you all I see that confidence has been replaced by anger and cynicism. The world has shrunk for you all. All you can do is go from home to college and then college to home. Is that what you want? Don't you want to experience more? Live more? Don't you want to be able to walk the streets as freely as I once did?" Zaira spoke from the heart and I could see that every word she uttered stirred something in the hearts of the young girls seated around her. She had shunned the stage they had set up for her and had, instead, asked for a chair and a mike. Then she asked the girls to sit around her in concentric circles. She wanted to be right among them.

"The onus of opposing Article 370 is actually on girls like you, because it is you who will lose certain rights if you get married outside Kashmir," Zaira went on. Then she took me completely by surprise with a confession I hadn't prepared myself for.

"I mean look at me. I love Vihaan and we plan to settle down together at some point in time. But thanks to Article 370, I will lose my right to buy property in Kashmir if I do that. In other words, its making me choose between land and the person I love. That, I think, is definitely not fair!"

Even as I stared at her, her words ricocheting inside my mind, the students immediately began teasing her.

"What would you prefer then, Ma'am? Being able to buy property in Kashmir or marrying Vihaan sir?"

"I prefer a new Kashmir, free from the burden of its past," was Zaira's prompt reply.

The entire hall gave her a thunderous applause.

Just as our car drove out of the college gate a little later, a motley group of about fifty young people surrounded us and started pelting stones at us. We were completely taken aback. Even as the policemen with us started getting out of their jeeps and tried to clear a path for our car to pass through, a huge group of girls from inside the college came out and completely took over the situation, challenging the stone-pelters to hit them instead of hitting our car. We couldn't believe what was unfolding in front of us. But as the girls stood around brazenly, the stone-pelters dispersed hastily.

Zaira and I got out of our car, stunned at the girls' bravery.

One of the girls walked up to Zaira and said, "Ma'am, I wish I can be like you. Elegant, intelligent and independent . . ."

Zaira hugged her, her eyes moist. "You are all of that, and more," she said, smiling.

Chapter Eleven: Srinagar, July 2017

Day 18, Baramulla

A lot had happened in the last six days. My friend, the rebel nationalist journalist, Pranab Goswami, whom I had met in Delhi, had executed the plan that I had proposed to him, launching a massive exposé that had blown the lid off of the whole system of funding of the Hurriyat leaders. The entire thing had been recorded on camera and played out, ad nauseam, for the whole country to see.

The top three Hurriyat leaders in the valley, including Zaira's father, had confessed on camera that they had received money from Pakistan's ISI on various occasions over the years for fanning trouble in the valley. They even had a rate card of sorts going! For a six month-contract for stone-pelting and other forms of violent disruptions, these Hurriyat leaders charged anywhere between INR 70 lakhs to INR 20 crores. The actual reward for say burning a government school or a police station was in the range of INR 50,000 and it would normally be shared by a team of six to eight people. The Hurriyat bosses, pocketing the difference after paying off the men on the ground, would thus make a mammoth profit on these assignments.

Needless to say, after the exposé was aired on various news channels across the country, these Hurriyat leaders disappeared completely. And when a TV channel pinned one of them, his cronies assaulted the channel's crew so badly that they were forced to run.

Exactly how Pranab had managed to actually act on the information I had provided to him and get the men to confess on tape were details I wasn't privy to, not that it mattered to me. I had wanted the job done and he had done exactly that. I had known that Zaira's father would be one of those who'd be caught in the exposé and I had grappled with the dilemma of whether to tell Zaira about it beforehand or not. But then Zaira herself had given up on her father. It wasn't for me to warn her of what was, clearly, an inevitable fate for him.

In the aftermath of this exposé, I found the people sobering down. The azaadi movement which they had been supporting and believing in for so long, now seemed more like a *dalali* (contractual business). A sense of having been betrayed dominated their psyche. This worked in my favour, for in my later interactions with the people, I found that they were ready to have a dialogue with me in my meetings.

In the Fatehpora village of Baramulla, not far from the Pakistan border, a group of nearly four-hundred youngsters came for an open discussion with me.

"But sir, hasn't India betrayed us by going back on the promise of conducting a plebiscite?" Yasin, a twenty-year-old college-goer, wanted to know.

I nodded, taking a minute to choose my next words carefully for I knew the answer wouldn't be that straight and easy to formulate. "Well . . . as per the commitment given by India to the United Nations, a plebiscite can be conducted only after the whole of Kashmir has been handed back to India. So, given that that has not happened yet, the very rationale of a plebiscite goes for a toss."

Murmurs of disagreement went around the crowd, but no one said anything out aloud as I continued. They all appeared a little unsure yet about how to react.

"But tell me this, since you raised the question of a plebiscite, why do you all keep insisting on this plebiscite when you all have been so fickle-minded throughout?"

Chapter Eleven: Srinagar, July 2017

I could see annoyed expressions on most faces in the crowd at my question. But I charged right ahead.

"I mean think about it. You never really wanted to be with Pakistan. Your heart wants azaadi while your mind knows that you're much better off with India. No matter the conditions under which you became a part of India, did you ever give India a fair chance? Did you ever completely embrace India? When you didn't, then why do you blame India alone for this trust deficit?"

"What do you mean we didn't give India a fair chance?" one of the students demanded, standing up and staring at me belligerently.

"Look at Article 370 . . . it was meant to be a temporary provision, wasn't it?" I shot right back. "How about removing it temporarily? Have you thought about that? Have you thought about letting India in? Just see the difference it makes if you put a temporary stay on Article 370. Just allow twenty per cent of the land area in the state to open up for settlement by outsiders and see the difference it will make in your lives. Reopen your cinema halls, start your own entertainment industry, make your own films and TV serials in Kashmiri. You will be amazed at the avenues it opens up for you."

Perhaps the youngsters realised that I was speaking from my heart, perhaps they sensed that there was no guile in my words, no subterfuge, because they responded to everything that I had said almost instantaneously. More than sixty per cent of the youngsters gathered there got together after our discussion got over and formed the Maqbool Sherwani Students Front with the intention of reviving and re-establishing a stronger connection with India. Zaira and I couldn't believe that the young people in front of us even remembered Maqbool Sherwani and were ready to resurrect him from his grave. It was incredibly reassuring that they, a part of the young Kashmir, were so open for a course correction.

It was in the midst of this unexpected revival of pro-India sentiments that I felt encouraged enough to add a small but significant twist to Vajpayeeji's original slogan of *Kashmiriyat, Jamhooriyat, Insaniyat*. I added the word 'Hindustaniyat' to it, explaining to the crowd around me how *Kashmiriyat, Jamhooriyat, Insaniyat* could thrive ideally only under the wider ambit of Indian nationhood. To my pleasant surprise, the crowd at Baramulla accepted this slogan. The public square where I had been speaking rang out with shouts of "*Kashmiriyat, Jamhooriyat, Insaniyat, Hindustaniyat!*"

As I turned around and looked at Zaira, standing right beside me all throughout, I knew it wouldn't take long for the slogan to evolve into a strategy. I could already sense it beginning to take hold, slowly but surely, in the hearts and minds of the people before me. I could feel that a new history wasn't impossible anymore.

Day 23, Srinagar

The final day of my reintegration yatra came upon me rather quickly. Where I had started off battling a hundred different doubts and uncertainties, the last few days had completely turned things around for us. The Baramulla slogan had reached all corners of the valley and evoked sharp reactions from the people, one way or the other. Surprisingly, a good percentage of the young people had lapped it up. More and more of them wanted to engage with me and understand what I had to offer. Of course, this had really shaken the Hurriyat and made them begin to feel insecure of my growing popularity. Intelligence agencies, quite naturally, were anticipating a big security threat to me.

I started the day by visiting the Gaw Kadal Bridge and observing a five-minutes-silence there. Fifty protestors had been massacred there on 21 January 1990 by the Indian paramilitary troops of the CRPF. In a place as complicated as Kashmir, I had to walk the tight rope. I hoped that this gesture would help the people of the valley shed their reservations about me and make them more open to everything that I had proposed so far.

Then I went back to Lal Chowk where it had all began with just fifty people. Now, as I made my way to the stage, I saw that there were no less than five-thousand people who had gathered. Not all of them were my supporters, but they were inquisitive about what I was up to and what I had to offer.

"Love and respect . . . that's all I have to offer to you besides the promise of a peaceful future," I told the gathering, opening the address.

I promised them the best of everything that any other part of India had. "But for that," I cautioned them, "the love and respect have to be mutual. Disputes within the family need not be exposed to a nosy and greedy neighbour."

I did not hesitate from spelling out my larger plan for the valley: a day when Kashmir represented a unique model of sustainable development for the world, where it hosted the world's topmost economic and sustainable development summits and gave close competition to Davos; a day when every village in Kashmir was connected by road and the best of educational institutes and hospitals had come up in remote areas of the valley.

Then someone asked me about Article 370. I nodded; I had

been anticipating that one. "Only you have the power to decide its fate, for the Constitution has vested that power in you. I can only convince you of the harm it has done to you. Progress requires a big heart. Just open up twenty per cent of your valley to outsiders and see the difference it makes to your life, see how it changes your worldview."

I couldn't have been more direct about what I felt about Article 370 and about Kashmir's self-imposed isolation. But I had been rather apprehensive about putting my opinion into words in front of such a huge crowd. I was expecting criticism and rejection, but in the expectant silence that followed my words, I realised that the people hadn't really taken an offence to what I had said. Instead, they appeared keen that I go on with what I had to say. I knew then that nothing was impossible if one's intentions were noble, if one's approach was that of love and respect, and most importantly, if one's political will was there, because if I were to hold any single factor responsible for reducing Kashmir to the cauldron of repressed anger and frustration that it was, it was the cumulative absence of political will of both the centre and the state.

Sensing the positive receptiveness of the crowd, I took the debate a step further.

"I have toured the valley extensively in these last twenty-three days and found that while most of those who protest against the government are people who are unhappy for want of better opportunities, there is a section that wants to impose the Shariat. There are people sitting right among you all who are fighting to install the Salafi version of Islam in Kashmir . . ." I paused, taking stock of the crowd's anticipation building up. More and more mobile phones were coming out as people began recording my speech.

Chapter Eleven: Srinagar, July 2017

"But there can't be a worse thing to happen to this beautiful valley than Salafi Islam taking roots in its soil. India has seen that before, under Aurangzeb, and India can't afford to see it again. Had it not been for Aurangzeb, at least half of you standing here would not be Muslims and the other half would perhaps be followers of Sufism, not Salafism."

My words stunned everybody in the crowd, including Zaira and my own self. I hadn't thought it wise earlier to touch upon this particular point in my closing speech. But perhaps that's the power of truth and of a heart which believes in that truth. It gives you the courage to not fear the repercussions of following what you believe in. I could see a section of the crowd getting restive, but I didn't care.

"Kashmir stands at a critical juncture today. And for the first time, the threat is not external, it is internal. The fight is about your thought process, it is about your beliefs. Today you have to make a choice between following the ideals of the great Sufi saint Noor-ud-Din Noorani or the bigotry of Aurangzeb. This choice is what will determine the future of Kashmir from here on—"

No sooner had I said this when a small section of the crowd started shouting: "Hindustan Zindabad! Hindustan Zindabad!" The very next moment, another small section of the crowd began shouting the slogan I had given at Baramulla: "Kashmiriyat, Jamhooriyat, Insaniyat, Hindustaniyat!"

I could clearly see the winds of change beginning to blow. However, the only thing certain about life is uncertainty. And the very next moment proved so.

All of a sudden, Zaira jumped in front of me and then she slumped forward, collapsing on the stage. It was only then that I realised that someone from the crowd had shot at me. Zaira, seeing it, had pushed herself in front of me in order to shield me and had taken the bullet herself.

In that fraction of a second, blood, fear, and chaos replaced every single bit of the optimism I had just begun to feel. Mayhem broke out in the crowd as people realised what had happened and started to run helter-skelter. My security detail rushed to form a protective cordon around us as I sat cradling Zaira's limp body in my lap, shouting for someone to get an ambulance, the warmth of Zaira's blood seeping through my clothes, chilling me.

***

Ten Days Later

It was the 15th of August and we had planned a human chain around Dal Lake as a show of strength of the pro-India forces in the valley to mark the occasion of our Independence Day. When I had first planned the event, I had imagined Zaira beside me, linking me to the valley in more ways than one. But ten days after sustaining two bullet hits in her rib area, she was still in the ICU, battling for her life. Somewhere along the line, as I moved between keeping a near-constant vigil outside the ICU and carrying on with the work I had set out to do, I had stopped feeling anything. Fear and dread had been replaced by a strange chill in my heart.

I had wanted to postpone the event, not wanting to leave Zaira alone even though she was heavily sedated almost all the time and was hardly conscious of my presence. But my party remained adamant; they reasoned that we couldn't afford to

Chapter Eleven: Srinagar, July 2017

let go of the momentum my reintegration yatra had created. Moreover, the attack had actually led to an immense wave of sympathy for Zaira and me. It had turned the public mood against the militants. Now even the otherwise wary chief minister, whom our party was supporting, was willing to join the human chain. We just couldn't let go of this opportunity.

A day before, I had been sitting beside Zaira in the ICU, feeling tense and incredibly lonely even though it had been a relatively better day for Zaira—she had been awake for a little while and had been responding to me in broken sentences and monosyllables. Perhaps she had sensed my despair, because she had gestured to me to tell her what the matter was.

"I don't know . . ." I said, shrugging my shoulders. "I am just feeling lonely . . . We had started this mission together, Zaira. I want to end it with you by my side."

Zaira just nodded. Then a minute or so later, she beckoned to me to come close. I shifted and brought myself closer to her. With gestures and stuttering words, she then proceeded to outline a plan which left me amazed at her sheer will power.

***

Dal Lake has a huge fifteen-kilometre-long circumference which virtually borders almost every part of Srinagar. Therefore, to have a human chain all around it means getting together at least fifty-thousand people. Half of this number was made up by supporters my party unit in the state had ferried from Jammu. The other half would be people who came on their own accord. But the local support was still lukewarm. It wasn't that people weren't prepared to embrace my idea of Kashmir. The real problem was that an open show of support for an Indian leader carried the threat of being disowned by the zealots of Kashmir. People were afraid to voice their opinions and take a stand openly. And hence, the number of local people was not in excess of eight to ten thousand.

As per Zaira's plan, I had gotten five giant LED screens installed at five key points along the lake so that she could address the people from her hospital bed. Her doctors and I had been reluctant to let her do something like this, but she had been adamant. Besides these giant screens, Pranab Goswami's news channel was also webcasting the whole event live so that everybody could watch it on their cell phones.

It was afternoon by the time we started the event and I welcomed everyone, thanking them for the overwhelming show of support. But I was subdued and distracted. Zaira's condition was playing at the back of my mind all the time.

When the time came for Zaira to go live from her hospital bed, I couldn't help but shudder. She had been talking to me in sporadic instalments of monosyllabic words and gestures. How could she pull off addressing such a huge crowd? But when she started, I found myself going absolutely still like everyone else in the crowd in front of me. All eyes were glued to the screens, to that pale, drawn face trying to smile bravely and talk. Zaira's voice was a hoarse whisper when she spoke and she took long pauses in between her words.

"Even now . . . ten days after taking the bullet . . . doctors have given me . . . only a fifty per cent chance . . . of survival . . ."

Long pause.

"But seeing . . . your enthusiasm, chances of Kashmir . . . surviving . . . are higher . . . as a daughter of Kashmir, I swear . . . India has not let you down . . . Those you trusted . . . in Kashmir . . . are the ones who have failed you . . ."

Chapter Eleven: Srinagar, July 2017

Even though her words were strained and unclear, the channel footage was simultaneously playing out captions of what she was saying. Every word, coming out laboured, was like a nail in the coffin of those who had wantonly played with the people of Kashmir.

"Allah has given you . . . a great chance to rewrite history. G-g-grab it . . ."

And then Zaira collapsed. The entire crowd was numb. No one reacted. No one broke the silence. But I ran. The fear of losing Zaira had me leave everything and run to the hospital. I couldn't imagine a new Kashmir or a new life for myself without Zaira.

Four hours later, I heaved a sigh of relief when Zaira's doctors told me that she had regained consciousness and that I could see her, but not for more than two minutes.

When I went in, Zaira looked paler still, but she smiled when she saw me. I couldn't trust myself to speak, not in that moment. I just walked up to her and kissed her softly on her forehead, thanking God for keeping her alive.

It was only much later in the night, when my secretary came to the hospital with some food and with my cell phone—I had given it to him just before going on stage to address the crowd—that I came to know about what had happened at Dal Lake after I had left the venue all helter-skelter and with the fate of our event hanging. In Mahesh's words, "something unthinkable had happened".

Pranab's channel had astutely played bytes from Zaira's speech repeatedly, especially the last part. So great was the impact of everything that had transpired that by evening, the number of people who had gathered all along the Dal Lake had swelled to over sixty-thousand. The emotionally charged crowd seemed prepared to embark immediately upon a conscious course correction. Chants of *Hindustan Zindabad* had echoed all around. As it grew dark, the crowd, instead of dispersing and going home, began forming their own sub-groups and thrashed out their own strategies to change the status quo. When they were asked to finally disperse, they took to patrolling the streets of Srinagar, shouting pro-India and anti-Pakistan slogans. When one compared this momentous night with that dreaded night of 19 January 1990, it was all but obvious that time had come a full circle. Never had Kashmir seen such a strong determination to purge itself of the arsenic clasp of Pakistan. Never had Kashmir seen so intense a call to cement its future with India.

When dawn broke, the most telling image of this change, and one that kept appearing all across the media, was of the tricolour flying proud and high in the cold morning wind in Lal Chowk, right in the heart of Kashmir.

As soon as I was informed of this, I rushed to the spot. Coincidentally, the chief minister arrived there roughly at the same time and we both stood in front of the flag, stunned by how things had turned out. I saluted the Indian flag, my eyes moist and a deep sense of fulfilment in my heart. I had pulled off a victory out of thin air. The path now seemed clear for Kashmir's marriage with India.

> 'Gar firdaus bar-rue zamin ast,
> hami asto, hamin asto, hamin ast'
>
> (If there is heaven on earth, it is here,
> it is here, it is here)
>
> **- Amir Khusro**

EPILOGUE

May 2030
7, Lok Kalyan Marg, New Delhi

It's a Saturday evening. I have just come out of my last meeting before the weekend finally sets in. The meeting was actually a discussion of the key agenda for us at the World Climate Summit scheduled for next week. India has taken a huge lead over the rest of the world in reducing its carbon footprint and I want to consolidate India's leadership. I have to now take one last look at the proofs of my first book. It's a work of non-fiction where I lay bare my thoughts on the rare renaissance that India seems to be witnessing as a nation. Needless to say, a big part of it has to do with my experience in Kashmir. I am calling it *Resurgent Paradise*. Everything is a little rushed now because the book's slated for a release in the next month. I am a bit distracted though, the way I am on a Saturday afternoon, thinking about Sunday.

I recently completed three years as the prime minister of India, one less than Zaira as the chief minister of Jammu and Kashmir. We live in different cities, naturally, she in Srinagar and I in Delhi. But we meet for exactly thirty-six hours every week, from late Saturday evening until the early hours of Monday morning. One weekend I travel to Srinagar and the other weekend she travels to Delhi. We miss each other all the time, but the dream that we share for India, the passion we feel for the country, it keeps us from despairing.

After our resounding success thirteen years ago in changing the political discourse in Kashmir, Zaira decided to stay back in Srinagar and contest the next Assembly elections. On the other hand, I was reinstalled as the defence minister, with my position strengthened manifold. Some sections of the media even began to view me as the PM's successor. In 2019, the PM decided to change my portfolio and shifted me from being the defence minister to being the home minister. The next year, in 2020, our party created history by forming its own government in Jammu and Kashmir. Zaira, now an MLA, was inducted as the cabinet minister for education. Right after her induction, after having known each other for about three decades, and four years into our 'revived' long distance relationship, Zaira and I got married in a small, private ceremony in Delhi.

We were perhaps destined to be together, yet distanced. In the initial years, Zaira's being in Srinagar and my being in Delhi irked me. I couldn't accept the fact that our relationship seemed doomed to be a perpetual long distance one. However, as we settled into our changed roles, both professionally and personally, I learned to take things in my stride and appreciate what I had.

Kashmir is now a tranquil place, much like it ought to have always been. Article 370, which had inhibited its complete integration into India, stands abrogated. However, its abrogation wasn't as satisfying as the fact that it happened through the will of the people, in a campaign driven largely by the women of the state. Zaira had personally toured every block of Kashmir and explained the merits and demerits of the Article for Kashmir. She had encouraged the people to be big-hearted and opt for sustainable, long-term gains rather than settle for limited, short-term ones. Though the people had their apprehensions, and quite naturally so, they eventually saw reason in our stand. For the ones who remained opposed to removing Article 370, we brought in a fresh law to safeguard their interests. According to this new law, the total land available for sale to non-residents in Kashmir could not exceed twenty per cent of the total land area available in the state. Furthermore, a native of Kashmir could buy a single piece of government land in any other state of the country at a subsidised rate. Incentives were provided for people in the valley to settle in Jammu and vice versa, in order to ensure that the two parts of the state did not resemble ghettos anymore. In fact, some 20,000 Kashmiri Pandit families have been resettled in the valley since then and they have been living peacefully in Kashmir.

The states of Jammu and Kashmir and Himachal Pradesh were restructured. Two districts of Himachal are now a part of J&K. This gargantuan change was made possible thanks to our party being in power in both the states and at the centre. A decision as path-breaking as this was bound to draw its share of flak. In historical retrospect, I am happy to bear this flak because I know that by creating a more evenly balanced demographic distribution within Jammu and Kashmir, I have saved the state from many future problems. I owe my decisions to my country and her future generations, not to a motley group of outdated journalists who consider me 'intolerant'.

Of course, we had to hard sell the idea of restructuring the state on the economic plank. I was ready to prove that the proposed restructuring was more like an economic package for

Jammu and Kashmir as it would boost the state's revenue by thirty-five per cent. But that's what good politics is: your real motives and the reasons you offer for public consumption need not be the same.

Kashmir has actually grown into an economic hub today. The GDP is up by more than three per cent in the last five years. Local businesses are thriving in all corners of the state. Moreover, Leh now hosts the prized Sustainable Development Summit every year, a unique three-day property in which over a hundred countries participate.

Most importantly, two years ago, POK broke away from Pakistan and declared its independence after a sustained armed struggle. I have no qualms in admitting that their secession was strategically supported by us. It was a calculated long-term risk that we took because we believed that a new state, formed with our support, would be grateful and friendlier to us. And so it turned out. Western Kashmir, as the new country is called, is anti-Pakistan and aligned with us on security issues. Together, we've successfully managed to almost eliminate terrorism from the valley.

There are a lot of things that have been accomplished in the years that have gone by and there is a lot that needs to be done still. But it's already close to six in the evening and I have to rush to the airport to catch the flight that will take me to Srinagar.

It will be well past nine by the time I get to see Zaira. As always, we will go for a shikara ride on the Dal Lake. It's a ritual between the two of us when I am in Srinagar. I know it will be especially magical today because it's going to be a full moon night. There will be a slight nip in the air and Zaira will sit close to me, putting her hands in the pocket of my jacket. We'll talk for a while but then we'll fall silent. Somewhere near the middle of this moonlit paradise, our shikara owner will start playing our favourite songs on his old transistor. He's the same man who had been shot when an assassination attempt had been made on me all those years ago. He's our shikara man, and we always go to him for these moments of quiet. I will lie down on the shikara, looking up at the stars above, and Zaira will rest her head on my chest. Our eyes closed, our hearts beating in harmony, we will hum along to the songs together. In that moment, for me and for Zaira, the world with all its madness and chaos will cease to exist and time will seem to freeze. It will be just me and her, two old souls in love.

And then, as the last of the songs dies out, in the softest of whispers, Zaira will recite one of her poems, the one that I love the most, the one that is etched in my heart:

> *This is the paradise I belong to*
> *The woods are my home and the trees my family*
> *Mountains my goals, rivers my path*
> *Snow my cushion and wind my friend*
>
> *This is the paradise I belong to*
> *And it is in the moment right now, with me in your arms*
> *that our heartbeats become one, singing the same song*
> *Our souls meet and follow the same path.*
>
> *This is the paradise I belong to*
> *Where illusions fade away and dreams become reality.*
> *After eluding each other for years,*
> *this is our moment of permanence*
> *Of a belongingness which even time can't snatch.*

An excerpt from *Resurgent Paradise*[1]

Sense and peace have returned to the valley. The *kahwa* has regained its pristine, native aroma; people look more energetic and vibrant. They call it New Kashmir, which rightly complements a new India. The Srinagar of 2030 is more like the Srinagar of 1930—purged of all violence and accommodating of diverse strands of life.

Even as a new chapter is being written in Kashmir, it won't be out of place to revisit history and remember the chain of unfortunate events that had led to Kashmir's fall into doom. Remembrance is, after all, the most basic shield against repetition. And for a generation which is largely flippant and inadequately informed, it is all the more important that they develop a good sense of history.

---

[1] *Resurgent Paradise* by Vihaan Shashtri (Fingerprint! 2030)

There are around half a dozen complicated developments that took place in the last seventy-odd years or so which explain the mess that Kashmir used to be. All of these situations are replete with unanswered questions. They will probably remain unanswered forever because the historical characters responsible for these situations are the only ones with the answers and they are, unfortunately, all long gone. And so, these answers that are so critical to the future of Kashmir, remain buried with them in their graves.

Much of Kashmir's problems emanate from the basic fact that for a land area that big, there are far too many ethnically diverse groups living within it. So, while the Kashmir valley comprised largely of Kashmiri Muslims with a small percentage of Kashmiri Hindu Pandits, in Jammu majority of the population was Dogra. Ladakh was Buddhist, while Gilgit and Balistan had a majority population of Dardi and Balti tribes. The areas of Muzzafarabad and Mir had a Punjabi-Muslim population, dissimilar from the valley Muslims.

The question that arises is how did a land so diverse exist homogenously as a single kingdom?

Jammu and Kashmir State was created for the first time with the signing of the Second Treaty of Amritsar between the British East India Company and Raja Gulab Singh of Jammu on 16 March 1846. It was an addendum to the Treaty of Lahore, which had been signed one week earlier, on 9 March 1846, and which defined the terms of surrender of the Sikh Darbar at Lahore to the British. The Sikhs, however, were unable to pay a part of the demand made by the British. Gulab Singh

An excerpt from Resurgent Paradise

stepped in on their behalf and paid INR 7,500,000, and in return, received the Kashmir valley, a region annexed by the Sikhs in 1820 from its Afghan rulers. The Kashmir valley, which Gulab Singh so acquired, was a Muslim majority-region, with its people speaking the Kashmiri language and having a distinct culture called 'Kashmiriyat'. Under Gulab Singh now, the Kashmir valley was added to the regions of Jammu and Ladakh, regions already under his rule.

Hence, strange as it may sound, the shape and geography of ancient kingdoms were largely the result of the territorial avarice of their rulers, and not so much of the actual composition of the population that lived there.

Therefore, in 1846, when the Dogra dynasty took over the reins of the entire state of Jammu and Kashmir, it was a clan that had been, until then, largely centred in the Jammu region. The new state of Jammu and Kashmir, however, now included Ladakh, Gilgit-Baltistan, Muzaffarabad-Mirpur, Aksai Chin and the Saksham valley, with feudatories like Hunza and Nagar. This, without a doubt, made it the most multi-cultural, multi-linguist, and multi-religious state of India.

The Sikh and then the Dogra regimes in Kashmir came in the aftermath of nearly a hundred-and-fifty years of Mughal and Afghan rule. To an extent, therefore, history was bound to reverse itself with a Hindu dynasty holding the reins of power and control. From the 1820s, there were reports of oppression of the Muslim majority in various forms, such as with the introduction of death penalty for cow slaughter and the imposition of higher taxes on them. The Hindu minority, on the other hand, was much favoured by the rulers and enjoyed preferential treatment in education and government jobs. This went on for nearly a hundred years. Things, however, got a lot better under the last Dogra ruler, Hari Singh, who took over the reins of Kashmir in 1925. Hari Singh was a progressive, largely non-partisan ruler who was a revolutionary social reformer and educationist.

However, the past reputation of the Dogra rulers overshadowed Hari Singh's performance, and Sheikh Abdullah, a young leader of the valley, exploited this shrewdly for his political benefit.

Sheikh Abdullah, along with Chaudhary Ghulam Abbas, formed the Muslim Conference in 1932 to champion the rights of the subjugated Muslims and to overthrow the princely rulers from the valley. In 1937, Abdullah met Nehru and both of them seemed to have instantly formed a mutual admiration society. This meeting led to Abdullah converting his crusade for 'Muslim interests' into one for 'national interests'. And so, the Muslim Conference was renamed the National Conference in 1939. The original Muslim Conference continued to exist as a rival, with its co-founder, Chaudhary Ghulam Abbas, at the helm of affairs.

The Nehru-Sheikh friendship marked the start of an intriguing political collaboration that was to run for generations between the two clans. While this friendship was crucial in securing Kashmir for India when the time came for the state to decide with which nation it wanted to side, India or Pakistan, in multiple ways, it was also

An excerpt from *Resurgent Paradise*

responsible for the crippled existence that Kashmir began to lead right after its accession to India.

In 1946, Sheikh Abdullah led a massive Quit Kashmir movement against Hari Singh. The movement was ill-timed, considering how close the country was to independence, but it was a show of strength on Abdullah's part. He clearly wanted to establish himself as the future leader of the valley.

Given the politically charged atmosphere in the country at that time, Abdullah was, quite naturally, jailed. After his election as Congress president, Nehru, who had once called Abdullah his 'blood brother', came out in full support of the jailed Abdullah and in June 1946, he decided to go to the valley to free him. This move was a serious blunder on Nehru's part. It antagonised Hari Singh completely, to the extent that one year later, despite being dead against the idea of joining Pakistan, he became reluctant to be a part of the Nehru-led India.

Nobody doubts Nehru's love for the country, but he was given to juvenile idiosyncrasies which were self-destructive and which often made his intellectualism appear as sham. A more concrete evidence of this was witnessed in his handling of the Indo-China war of 1962.

In a letter to D. P. Mishra, an exasperated Patel, a more capable leader, had this to say about Nehru: 'He [Nehru] has done many things recently which have caused us great embarrassment. His actions in Kashmir . . . are acts of emotional insanity and it puts tremendous strain on us to set the matters right.' However, Patel, always fair, added: '. . . but in spite of all these innocent indiscretions he has unparalleled enthusiasm and a burning passion for freedom.' Patel thus pointed out the two conflicting traits in Nehru that more often than not, squandered away his good intentions.

To be fair to Hari Singh, left with no options and aware of the looming threat of an incursion from across the border, the Maharaja made an offer to join India in September 1947. This offer, however, was not entertained by Nehru, who first demanded the release of Sheikh Abdullah. Hari Singh, pushed into a corner by Nehru and Abdullah, was to now become somewhat 'delusional' and preferred Kashmir's independence. Moreover, Nehru didn't want to lose control over the handling of Kashmir to Patel within the party.

Kashmir's accession to India, as we well know it, happened under unusual conditions. On 22 October 1947, weeks after Independence, Pakistan unveiled its non-state actors for the first time, when it fronted tribal armies from the North West Frontier Province to invade Kashmir. This was a violation of the Standstill Agreement that the Maharaja had already signed with Pakistan. And hence, given the magnitude of the invasion, Hari Singh had only two options left—either to let the entire kingdom go to Pakistan or join India and let the Indian army battle it out. The Maharaja chose the latter.

On 26 October, therefore, the Instrument of Accession was executed by the Maharaja, and Kashmir became a part of India. On 27 October, Indian troops landed in Sringar even as Sheikh Abdullah himself organised private armies to support the Indian Army. The result was that the Pakistani non-state actors were pushed

An excerpt from Resurgent Paradise

back significantly, even though a good portion of the state to its west and north was still occupied by them.

While Hari Singh continued to hold the title of king for a few years succeeding Kashmir's accession to India, Sheikh Abdullah was installed as the Prime Minister of Kashmir. There was, however, a marked difference in the way that Hari Singh and Sheikh Abdullah viewed Kashmir's accession to India. While Hari Singh largely saw it as an unconditional move, Abdullah reiterated that it was a provisional move and that the actual fate of Kashmir would be subsequently decided by the will of the people. Abdullah's stand led him to constantly bargain with and blackmail the Indian establishment for favours which were exceptional and which, in reality, only ensured that Kashmir's integration with the rest of the nation remained incomplete. Article 370 and Section 35A, which were introduced subsequently to reassure the people of the valley that the spirit of Kashmiriyat that defined them would not be tampered with, are classic examples of how Kashmir went on to become a perpetual bargain deal for India.

Who is, therefore, to be blamed for Kashmir's messy accession to India? Should it be Nehru, Hari Singh or Sheikh Abdullah? From the facts that are available, it is apparent that Nehru and Abdullah were caught in a web of mutual machinations to secure their respective positions. So while Nehru had hoped that mollifying Abdullah would make him bend from his position and allow a smooth transition, Sheikh Abdullah, on the other hand, seemed to have been under the illusion that by supporting Nehru, and by extension India, at the critical point in 1947, India would subsequently allow self-determination for Kashmir. But that was never India's stated stand. Sheikh Abdullah was living a delusional notion of independence, much like Hari Singh himself, after a point. Moreover, Abdullah's crusade for independence was largely the result of his avarice for political glory, as became evident through various developments that took place over the next three decades.

***

Another critical development that ensured that Kashmir remained entangled in conflict was Nehru's hasty decision to refer the dispute to the United Nations Security Council on 1 January 1948. He is supposed to have been persuaded by Lord Mountbatten, who urged his wife, Edwina, with whom Nehru was supposedly involved romantically, to convince Nehru to take the matter to the United Nations. Nehru, apparently, was also promised the support of Britain at the United Nations. But Britain betrayed India with its pro-Pakistan stand in the U.N. The battle to flush out the Pakistani invaders continued till November 1948, but the hostile climate and the difficult terrain of the valley were proving to be a big deterrent for the Indian troops. Besides, there were other big challenges like Hyderabad and the North East where these troops were needed. And hence, on 31 December 1948, a formal ceasefire was declared in the valley.

Now, Nehru could have had various motives in agreeing to leave one-third of Kashmir as disputed territory in the control of the enemy. Perhaps he may have realised that the ethnic majority of this 'disputed' part of Kashmir would anyway make it extremely difficult for India to govern it. After all, the deep pockets of influence that tribal gangs from the North West Front Province had in this region had been a shocking eye-opener for the Indian establishment.

Over the next few years, as independent India settled into tackling the numerous challenges facing it, it could have made a concerted effort to claim POK back through military force. But then, this period also corresponded with the dawning of new realities, and the same Sheikh Abdullah who had once been seen as a leader of the people of Kashmir, now emerged as a wily blackmailer. It was as a part of Abdullah's bargaining demands and Nehru playing ball to them, that Article 370 was incorporated into the Indian Constitution, thus according a dangerously special status to the state. Article 370 was supposed to be a temporary provision only, in that its applicability was intended to last till the formulation and adoption of the state's constitution. However, the state's Constituent Assembly dissolved itself on 25 January 1957 without recommending either the abrogation or the amendment of Article 370. And like our caste-based Reservation policy, which too was a short-term provision, Article 370 became a permanent weapon for the political parties of the state to wield in the face of the Indian government.

Of course, in due course of time, India realised its folly in letting Article 370 be and through various presidential orders, the act was considerably diluted over the years. But the fact that no outsider could buy land in the state isolated it from the positive and progressive influences from other parts of the country. The Article provided just the apt breeding ground for fundamentalist forces which were all prepared to ransack the state in the years to come.

Nehru had finally realised his folly in backing Abdullah as early as 1953. In fact, by then, Abdullah had revealed his true colours and was increasingly seen as an embarrassment by the Indian leadership. His hobnobbing with Pakistan to extract more advantages from India was an open trick. Therefore, in August 1953, anticipating that Abdullah would launch a fresh azaadi movement to break free from India, Abdullah was dismissed as prime minister by Dr. Karan Singh, the then Sadr-e-Riyasat (Constitutional Head of Kashmir). Abdullah's deputy, Bakshi Ghulam Mohammad, was then installed as the PM of Kashmir.

In his radio speech after assuming office, the new PM of Kashmir had this to say about Sheikh Abdullah, "A fraud was being committed on the interests of the country. The slogan of independence was dangerous. Under the control of an imperialist power, an independent Kashmir would have been a serious danger for the people of India and Pakistan . . ."

Sheikh Abdullah was subsequently arrested and he remained in prison for the next ten years, until just months before his death, the Indian PM, in an almost whimsical manner, withdrew all cases against Abdullah and had him released from jail.

The ten years that Abdullah spent in prison were perhaps the best years for Kashmir. The new PM, even

An excerpt from *Resurgent Paradise*

though he steadfastly guarded Kashmir's special status, proved himself to be a deft administrator. The state took rapid strides in education and public infrastructure. Even though Abdullah's supporters carried out some propaganda activity under a new front called the Plebiscite Front, Bakshi dealt with law and order issues with an iron hand. Kashmir saw one of its most peaceful phases during this time.

On his release from jail, Abdullah proved himself to be a more wily politician, and this time round, he refused to budge from his demand of a plebiscite. And hence, when Nehru died in 1964, his successors were left with a new set of problems to battle in the valley.

Soon after Nehru's death, Abdullah was interned from Kashmir for eighteen months and his Plebiscite Front was banned from taking part in the elections. Right after this, the National Conference was dissolved and merged with the Indian National Congress in a marked centralising strategy. With the Congress now ruling both at the centre and in the state, it was a great opportunity for the Indian government to integrate Kashmir with the rest of the country fully and thus conclusively end its problems. But the government of the day lacked the political will power required.

Instead, a much mellowed Abdullah made another comeback to the centre of things in 1975. The Indira Gandhi-Sheikh Abdullah pact paved the way for him to become the chief minister of the state. Even though in this last innings of his, Abdullah was conspicuously reconciliatory, what his restoration to power did was to make it easier for his deceptive legacy to continue.

After his death in 1982, his naive and flamboyant son, Farooq Abdullah, took over as chief minister of the state almost as a matter of natural ascension.

India had four decades to settle the problems of Kashmir internally, even if the external border dispute continued with Pakistan. But the Indian leadership's over-dependence on the National Conference kept it in a state of complacence and denial. The result was that power in the state was centred within a small cartel, leading to the fundamentalist fringe growing exponentially and posing the biggest challenge to the country by the mid-1980s.

What is also noteworthy is that despite Kashmir never being short on budgetary allocations from the centre, the Abdullahs were, quite clearly, poor administrators. Roads and infrastructure were never their remotest priorities. Instead, instigating the people of Kashmir against India and bargaining endlessly with the Indian leadership seemed to be their prime agenda.

To be fair to Farooq, though, when he took over, his politics was more mainstream than his father's. He was more aligned to Kashmir's future being with India than his father ever had been. This could have stemmed from his own ambitions of emerging as a national leader, but it was sufficient to rile an insecure Congress, which had, by then, become subservient to Indira Gandhi's whims and fancies.

In 1984, the elected majority government of Farooq Abdullah was dismissed by the governor, Jagmohan, who combined the virtues of being an able administrator with that of being a stooge of Mrs. Gandhi. G. M. Shah, an

An excerpt from *Resurgent Paradise*

inept man who happened to be the estranged brother-in-law of Farooq, was installed as the new chief minister of the state.

By 1986, however, Shah's all-round failure led to his government being dismissed, and in a dramatic turn of events, Farooq, who had begun to encourage anti-India forces in the valley, and the Congress, which had been calling the National Conference an anti-national body, got together for another unholy collaboration which came to be known as the Rajiv-Farooq Accord of 1987.

It is said that those who fail to learn from history are doomed to repeat it. This couldn't have been truer than in the case of Kashmir. The 1984 dismissal and the subsequent resurrection of Farooq Abdullah was reminiscent of the way his father had been dismissed in 1953, only to be reinstated later in 1975. There was, however, a marked difference between 1953 and 1984. In 1953, Sheikh Abdullah's blackmail had kept India on the edge. Farooq, on the other hand, couldn't exactly be accused of any such abuse of power in 1984.

The pact between Farooq Abdullah and Rajiv Gandhi shocked the people. They felt cheated because it sent out a clear message—that the politics of both the Congress and the National Conference was nothing but mere posturing that they cared two hoots for the fate of the Kashmiris.

The announcement of the pact led to a massive consolidation of fundamentalist Islamic forces in the valley, as they got together to fight the elections under the Muslim United Front (MUF). But the elections were rigged by the National Conference and Farooq returned to power.

It did not take time for many leaders of the MUF to pick up arms against India. The uncertainly and chaos of 1987 was, therefore, to turn into armed militancy of the worst kind in the years that followed.

What followed was the mass exodus of Kashmiri Pandits from the valley in 1989, leading to the doomed and catastrophic night of 19 January 1990, when slogans of azaadi and calls for the cleansing of the valley of its Kashmiri Pandit population rent the air. That night witnessed the worst ethnic cleansing in independent India, the scars of which remain unhealed till date in many Kashmiri Pandit homes.

Two days later, in a retaliatory action, about fifty unarmed protestors were shot dead by the Central Reserve Police Force on the Gaw Kadal Bridge.

Farooq Abdullah resigned immediately after the Gaw Kadal massacre and returned to active politics only when the democratic process was revived in the valley in 1996.

The deadly chain of militant attacks in the valley that followed and the brutal retaliation by the Indian army led to Kashmir being doomed to a perennially disturbed state. It also led to a whole generation of children growing up in the shadow of violence and hatred.

The situation improved significantly from 2002 onwards when a People's Democratic Party-led government took over the reins of the state, supported by the Bharatiya Janta Party. The then prime minister, Atal Bihari Vajpayee, had coined the famous slogan of

'Kashmiriyat, Jamhooriyat, Insaniyat' to sum up the essence of his stand on the issue of Kashmir. He explained to the Parliament that "issues can be resolved if we are guided by three principles of Kashmiriyat (Kashmir's age-old legacy of Hindu-Muslim amity), Jamhooriyat (Democracy) and Insaniyat (humanism)." The Vajpayee government was largely flexible and open to talks with all the stake-holders in the valley. In fact, the slogan was meant to be a part of the larger strategy that Vajpayee had in mind to solve the Kashmir dispute.

Even though Kashmir moved briskly towards peace and stability under Vajpayee's vision, the BJP government itself was soon voted out in 2004.

ACKNOWLEDGEMENT

My first book, *That Thing Called Love*, was released on 25 September 2006. In this journey of eleven-and-a-half years now, which begun rather serendipitously, this is my tenth book in all. They include three urban relationship sagas, four socio-political thrillers (with romantic inspiration), a thriller based in the world of cricket, a parenting book, which is perhaps India's first parenting book written from a father's point of view, a co-authored non-fiction development-politics narrative and a digital book.

It has been an exciting journey, replete with adventure and evolution, and one which would not have been possible without the love, support and faith of the lakhs of unknown readers who have read my books. I say lakhs because my first book has sold (fortunately or unfortunately) many times more as a pirated copy than as an original!

Some of my readers have made their way into my life—one is my spouse now, and a few others, my friends. Over the years, social media has made it easier to stay connected with readers and well-wishers than it used to be all those years ago when I started writing. I remain indebted to my huge family of known and unknown, visible and invisible readers and well-wishers across the globe.

I am grateful to Kanishka Gupta, Shikha Sabharwal, Gayatri Goswami, and Pooja Dadwal. As my literary agent for the book, publisher, and editors, all of you have been brilliant and extremely supportive.

In the process of writing this book, I spoke extensively to people connected with Kashmir and to those who have followed its social and political developments closely. That these people belonged to different walks of life and different ideologies only helped in getting varied perspectives. I am thus grateful to Tahir Syeed, a young PDP leader in Kashmir, Ratan Sharda, an RSS ideologue, and Raman Koul, a senior IT professional in Pune, who grew up in Kashmir. Saloni Kelam, a dear friend, had connected me to Raman, her cousin, for which I remain thankful.

The female protagonist of this book, Zaira, is a passionate poet and a professional writer. I have used several original poetic creations to bring out her thoughts at different points in the story. Five of these poems have been created by a dear friend and former colleague, Bhavna Berry. One of them (Page 115) has been created by fellow author and friend, Sujata Parashar. I remain thankful to them for this invaluable contribution.

This book has been written and edited amidst great professional and personal challenges. The writing coincided with my foray into active politics, and that imposed stiff demands on time. Hence, this is perhaps my first book which I have partly written and edited on flights. The editing coincided with a phase when my mother was seriously ill and later, passed away.

I remain grateful to my wife, Koral, my son, Neev Tanish, Daddy, and all my close family members who have been my pillars of strength throughout.